TOP SE

WARTIME JOURNAL

of

EVACUATED
NELLIE

ABOUT THE AUTHOR

Trisha Morris used to be a primary school teacher but now tutors part-time. She spends the rest of her time writing and drawing, and playing with her grandchildren. She also produced a magazine called Hilda Matilda and Friends. She lives in a wonky cottage in the middle of the Kent countryside with her husband, dog and chickens. She truly believes that she has fairies living in her garden.

Find out what happens to Nellie in the next instalment, "WARTIME NELLIE - BACK IN THE THICK OF IT!", coming soon!

THE
TOP SECRET
WARTIME JOURNAL
of

EVACUATED
NELLIE

ISBN 979 8 6003 1133 6

Ovaltine is a registered trademark of Associated British
Foods

For my mum,
Annie Willsher

Still up to mischief!

I know today is a strange time to start
writing a journal. You're supposed to start
them at the very beginning of the year, on
January 1st, but my teacher, Miss Robinson,
has given me a brand new exercise book, and
has told me that if I want to be a serious
writer I should practise writing every day,
and a journal is a good way of doing that.

Anyway, as my mum always says, when we're
charging down the road to school at half-past
nine in the morning, still ramming bread and
dripping into our mouths, 'better late than
never!'

Here are 3 facts about me:

Fact number 1   My name is Eleanor Jane
Walker, but most people
call me Nellie. This was because when I was
a baby my dad used to hold me in his arms and
sing his favourite song:

You're my heart's desire, I love you, Nellie Dean ...

The name sort of stuck, which is unfortunate
because my brother Frank calls me Smelly

1

Nellie, and now, so do all the boys at
school. I got the word UNFORTUNATE from the
dictionary Miss Robinson gave me. It means,
'worse luck'. I love words, which is why I
want to be a writer and also an illustrator
one day, like Beatrix Potter, which is, of
course …

Fact number 2

I don't want to write
about animals that talk,
and dress in jackets and
hats though. I want to write about the Wild
West, and cowboys and Indians.
I'm practising drawing horses at the moment
but they're really hard.

When my books are published I will
be known by my proper dignified
name, Eleanor Jane
Walker. Or possibly EJ
Walker, so people won't
know if I'm a girl or a
boy. Or even Dame
Eleanor Walker – that
will be once I am rich and
famous and become friends
with the king. Then people will pay me lots
of money to read my life story, which is the
other reason why I'm writing about my life
now - before I grow really old and forget all
the details.

My first novel is called DESERT HERO, because it's set in the Arizona desert. It's going to be made into a film, starring my absolute favourite film star, Johnny Mack Brown. He's been in lots of westerns so I know he'll be happy to star in mine.

We go and see them most Saturday mornings at the penny pictures. I'm not keen on the soppy kissing stuff in westerns, but it seems that you need to have it in there because that's what the grown-ups like. We always boo and hiss and make gagging noises like we're being sick when Johnny kisses the leading lady.

My novel's main character is called Tex (Johnny Mack Brown) and he is a cowboy. It begins with Tex rescuing a damsel in distress after her horse bolts. He rides alongside and brings the horse to a standstill.

3

> "Oh Tex!" The woman cried. "You're my hero"
> "Shucks, it was nothing," replied Tex,
> sweeping her up into his arms and planting a
> big smackeroony right on the lips...
>
> Desert Hero

There, that's the soppy stuff out of the way. Now I can move on to all the good fighting bits.

Miss Robinson says that a writer always uses their own experiences in their novels, and although I'm not actually a cowboy, and I certainly haven't kissed a boy (errgghh!) she says that I should include things that really happen to me.

Fact number 3 For quite a long time I've had something wrong with my legs. They don't look like everyone else's.

This was me when I was young:

This is what I should have looked like:

This is what I actually looked like:

Lovely straight legs

big knobbly knees

awful CALLIPERS

small and dainty Mary Jane shoes

huge gallumping boots

The nice picture on the left isn't true for more than one reason: I've never had pretty Mary Jane shoes like these, and the dress isn't actually mine. It's one that Mary O'Reilly owns (Mary O'Reilly's my friend). It's royal blue with a white Peter Pan collar. I'd like to have a dress like it one day though. But the bow is really mine - it's a lovely dark blue velvet one that I wear to church on Sundays.

The doctor says I had an illness called RICKETS which made my legs go like this. My knees were really knobbly and hurt when I walked. It's because I didn't have enough calcium, which you get in milk, and vitamin D, which you get from sunshine and oily fish.
   The trouble with milk is that you need a lot of it when you have a family as big as ours, and it's hard to make sure everyone has enough. But the sunshine is free when the sun bothers to come out, although our street is mostly in the shade from the rows of houses that stand all the way up and down it.
   Because of the Rickets I had to go to the hospital and the doctor put callipers on my legs.
When the doctor first told me, I thought he said 'CATERPILLARS!! I was horrified!
   'Will they be hairy?' I wailed. 'I don't want hairy caterpillars crawling up my legs!'
   'Not caterpillars,' the doctor said. 'Callipers. They're braces that we strap to your legs and, in time, your legs will be lovely and straight like everyone else's.'
He also said that I had to drink cod liver oil on a spoon every day (DISGUSTING!) as well

as having special milk which has vitamins added to it (fine by me).

The callipers were *awful* and the children at school laughed at me when I wore them, although I was used to that because they'd always laughed at my bandy legs anyway.

But one day my brother Frank had had enough of everyone teasing me. He stood next to me and began to wave his fists madly like a prize boxer, shouting, 'If anyone laughs at my sister any more they'll get one of these in the kisser, RIGHT?'

It seemed to do the trick because people weren't so bad after that.

Frank is always getting into fights for different reasons, and he usually wins. He can be really horrible to me at home sometimes, but it's nice having someone to stick up for you when you really need them.

The good news is that I had the callipers taken off last week and my legs are nearly normal. My left knee's still got a bit of a knobble, but my right knee's looking pretty good. My doctor has said that my left one will sort itself out in time if I keep drinking the vitamin milk and taking the cod liver oil. (Yuk!)

I often imagine I'm the main character in my own imaginary novel and everyone else around me, eg my family and friends, are the not so important characters.

At the moment I'm starring in an imaginary novel called "NELLIE IN WARTIME DANGER". This is because our prime minister, Neville Chamberlain, announced on the wireless last September that we were at war with Germany again. Not just us in England but all of Britain and half of Europe too. The news didn't come as a great surprise to anyone because we'd been preparing for war for months before. But since the announcement we haven't seen any Germans, not even the sound of one tiny German plane in the distance

I know that things are happening in Europe because we see films of the fighting when we go to the pictures, but all we do here is wait and prepare for action. It's like Britain is holding its breath, but it's gone all blue in the face from not breathing out for so long, so I think I might just change the title to "NELLIE NOT ACTUALLY IN WARTIME DANGER YET".

I am now going to introduce you to my cast of supporting characters (my family).

MY DAD (WILLIAM WALKER)

I've drawn my dad in his soldier's uniform because that's what he was wearing when I last saw him. He fought in the First World War, and his job was to look after the soldiers' horses. He won lots of medals for being so brave.

This time he volunteered to go to war, but we don't know what he's up to. They're not allowed to say. Everything has to be kept secret in case the Germans find out.

MY MUM (JANE WALKER)

My mum is a tiny little lady with a tiny little voice, but she has a BIG ferocious temper, and if we're naughty she chases after us and hits us with her slipper. I've often been caught on the backside with it, and it *hurts!*

If I had to use one word to describe her, it would be TIRED.

She spends all day looking after us children, or cleaning the house, or cooking the meals, or washing and drying the clothes. She also does washing for other people and they pay her for it.

On Friday evenings she goes to some people's houses called JEWS and lays their fires for them, ready for the next day, which is a special day for them called the SABBATH. They're not allowed to do any work on that day because God says you should have a rest. I think my mum could do with a rest.

MY BIG BROTHER, GEORGE WALKER

George works at our local docks delivering fish to the posh hotels in the West End of London. He's *mad* about motorcycles and would like one more than anything, but Mum won't let him have one because she's frightened he'll kill himself on it. At the moment he has a push bike, which I'm not allowed to ride, worse luck.

MY SISTER, JEAN WALKER

This is my eldest sister, Jean. Jean is incredibly beautiful and glamorous. She wants to be a film star in Hollywood one day. She works in a posh clothes shop, also in the West End, and is sometimes a model. She's always doing her hair and wears loads of make-up even if she's just popping out for a bag of chips.

'You never know, a Hollywood film director might secretly be out looking for a new leading lady for his latest film,' she says, tapping the side of her powdered nose.

'Oh yeah Jean,' I say, 'a famous Hollywood film director is really going to be hanging around our chip shop. All that lovely smelly vinegar!'

'Clear off, you cheeky beggar!' she laughs, pretending to clip me round the ear. I really love Jean.

MY NEXT BROTHER, FRANK WALKER

I've already told you that Frank likes a good punch-up. He's the one that calls me names and teases me a lot. He calls me a flaming nuisance, just because I always want to play with him.

'Why don't you get lost, Nellie?' he says grumpily. 'You're like a pesky wasp, buzzing around me all the time!'

I probably do buzz around him a lot, but it's only because he does such interesting things, and my life is mostly *boring* most of the time.

I really must tell you about the time Frank and his mates played the best game of "Knock-Down Ginger" ever played by anyone.

This is how you play Knock-Down Ginger normally:

1. Make sure there are no grown-ups about.

2. Knock on somebody's door and then quickly go and hide somewhere where you can still see the door.

3. The person comes out and looks around, wondering who knocked on their door.

4. When they've gone back inside, go and knock on their door again, and go back to your hiding place and wait for them to come out again.

5. Don't do it more than twice, because they'll catch on it's a kid playing a trick and they'll be ready for you the third time. Then you'll be in BIG trouble!

It's great fun. We love doing it to Grumpy Grover. He's a man who lives a few houses down from us. We often play tricks on him, but he always falls for it and then he gets so angry, he shakes his fist in the air and his face turns purple as if he's about to explode! And when he shouts you can see his one remaining bottom tooth, which is all black and mouldy. The rest of his teeth have already fallen out. He is truly a horrible sight.

One day Frank and his friends, Dave Holland, Paddy Mahoney and Johnny Doyle, played an extra ingenious version of Knock-Down Ginger. Frank found a long piece of thick string at the rubbish dump, so they tied it to Grumpy Grover's letterbox and also to the letterbox of the house next door to him. (Mrs Carey's house). Frank took hold of the other end of the string and they all ran and hid behind the dustbins. Frank then pulled the string and it knocked really loudly on Grumpy's knocker AND Mrs Carey's knocker at the same time. Rat-a-tat-tat!

This is where I came into the story. I'd just been doing an errand for Mum when I spotted them and ran over, really excited, and squatted down next to them.

'What are you doing, Frank?' I whispered. Frank wasn't very happy to see me. 'Go away Nellie,' he hissed at me. 'You're going to spoil it.'

'She's all right,' Dave said. 'Anyway, if we don't let her hide with us now, she might give the game away.'

At that moment Grumpy tried to open his door *and* so did Mrs Carey, but they couldn't because they were tied together. Every time Grumpy managed to pull his door open a bit further, then Mrs Carey's door would slam shut. Then she would yank hers open and Grumpy's door slammed shut. It was like watching a door see-saw. Open – shut – open - shut. And each time, their faces were getting redder and angrier.

'Will you shut your door, woman!' he shouted at Mrs Carey.

'No, you shut yours,' she replied. 'I want to open mine!'
It was so funny I nearly wet myself.

Suddenly Grumpy Grover disappeared and then his front window flew open. He climbed through it, jumped out and began following the string.

'He's spotted us!' Frank whispered to the others. 'Let's scarper!' He held out the rest of the string to me. 'You look after this for us, Nellie,' he said.

WHAT DO YOU THINK HAPPENED NEXT?

This is what should have happened:

"What do you think I am, stupid?" says Nellie and cleverly runs off before she is caught, leaving Frank (quite rightly) to get the blame.

This is what actually happened:

"Alright then," says Nellie in a gormless voice and takes the string, while Frank and his gang all run off and leave her.

The next thing I knew, Grumpy Grover's purple, angry face loomed over the dustbins and caught me red-handed.

'So it's you, you 'orrible little monster,' he shouted, his black tooth waggling away wildly. 'I might have known … disturbing decent people in their homes … you're nothing but trouble, you and that family of yours!'

I didn't tell on Frank and the others though, even when Grumpy Grover grabbed me by my ear and marched me to our house. He banged loudly on our door knocker and Mum came out.

'You need to keep this girl of yours under control!' shouted Grumpy Grover, and then told Mum what had happened, or what he *thought* had happened.

'Yes, thank you Mr Grover,' said Mum stiffly, removing my ear from Grumpy's grasp.

'I'll see that she's punished.' Then she turned to me, 'Now say sorry to Mr Grover, Nellie.'

'Sorry,' I mumbled.

'And that you won't play any more tricks, Nellie,' Mum continued.

'I won't play any more tricks.'

'Make a promise, Nellie,' said Mum.

'I promise.'

I wasn't allowed to go to the penny pictures on Saturday morning and I had to play Mums and Dads with our Maureen all day as a punishment. I don't know why I didn't tell on Frank — it's just that there's a sort of rule everyone knows: you don't blab on your mates — not that Frank is my mate. He was grateful though, and he gave me one of the sweets he bought with his pocket money. I didn't get any pocket money that week as part of my punishment.

Dave Holland came to see me. 'Thanks for not telling on us,' he said. 'That was a really decent thing you did there. The lads and I got together and had a bit of a whip-round for you.' He put his hand in his pocket and took out six more sweets, a piece of string, a little toy aeroplane and a rabbit's foot. 'This is my lucky charm that I'm giving you,' he told me, handing over the rabbit's foot. 'It hasn't got fleas or anything. It'll bring you good luck.' He patted the top of my head. 'You're a good sort, Nellie.'

It's nice to be appreciated by some people.

OUR MAUREEN
My youngest sister. I don't know who first started calling her '*our*' Maureen. It's not as if she looks like anyone else's Maureen, and that mum might mistakenly bring home the wrong Maureen from school one

day. Our Maureen has blonde, curly hair, a smiley, pretty face, and is so nice to everybody all the time. Everyone loves her. You would have thought that she would be annoying to be around, being so perfect, but if I'm horrible to her I feel really guilty afterwards because she doesn't fight back. Still, I *loathe* it when mum says I have to play with her, because all she wants to do is play mums and dads, which involves wrapping up dollies in blankets and having cups of pretend tea, or going to pretend shops. It's so boring!

This is one of the games I have to play with her. I've written it like a play because we're doing them at school at the moment:

Mums and Dads
Written and directed by Maureen Walker

Cast:
The mummy - played by our Maureen
The aunty that comes to visit - Me
The baby - our Maureen's favourite dolly, Edna Daffodil

Scene 1
The mummy's house.

(The mummy is busy making the tea.   Edna Daffodil has just had a bottle of pretend baby milk and is sleeping peacefully in a shoe box, wrapped in a tea cloth.
The aunty knocks at the pretend door.)
The mummy: Who is it?   *(She's wearing Mum's scarf, folded into a triangle and knotted under the chin, and a pair of Jean's high heels.)*
The aunty: It's me.
The mummy: Who's me?
The aunty: Get up and open the door, Dopey, and you'll find out.
(The mummy pretends the aunty hasn't called her a horrible name and she opens the imaginary door.)
 The mummy: Hello Aunty, come on in.   I've just made some lovely tea, just sit down there and I'll get you a cup.
(The aunty sits on a pretend chair.
The mummy pours tea from a pretend teapot and the aunty pretends to drink it with her little finger sticking out in a posh way.)
The mummy *(in a posh voice)*:   Isn't the weather nice out today?
The aunty *(also in a posh voice)*:   Not bad, considering there's six feet of snow outside, a terrifying hurricane blowing at the windows and thunder and lightning banging and crashing in the sky.   Yes, not bad at all.

No matter how much I try and make it a bit more exciting, it's just *boring, boring, boring!*

Last time we played Mums and Dads, my younger brothers, Peter and Paul, charged in like a pair of thuggish whirlwinds and grabbed Edna Daffodil out of our Maureen's arms.

'Look, the baby's cold,' said one of them, ripping Edna Daffodil's tea-towel off and chucking it on the floor.

'Let's put it in the oven and warm it up a bit,' the other one said in a wicked voice.

Our Maureen screamed, 'Give me Edna Daffodil back! Mum, Mum! Tell them to stop it!'

Mum charged in waving her slipper at them. 'Get outside you two, otherwise you'll get this across your backsides and you won't be able to sit down for a week!'

I used that moment to sneakily slip away and run off down the street. Phew! Safe at last!

Edna Daffodil

And that story brings me nicely (or not!) onto my twin brothers …

PETER AND PAUL

They are named after Saint Peter and Saint Paul, who were friends of Jesus, but saints they definitely are not! Because they're identical twins, people find it really hard to tell them apart - me included. I'm not sure Mum always knows either. They're constantly running around, shouting and breaking things, and are up to mischief twenty four hours out of every single day of the year.

THE BABY

Lastly we have the baby. He's actually called Daniel Patrick Neville Walker, but we just call him the baby. He doesn't seem to mind. I don't think he can speak English yet. He doesn't have much of a personality at the moment – all he does is sleep, cry or feed. I'm not in a hurry for him to grow up, just in case he turns out like the twins.

This is how we have prepared for the Germans coming:

Preparation No. 1

After the prime minister, Neville Chamberlain, told us about the war we all had to queue up and be fitted for a gas mask. They're in a cardboard box that you have to wear round your neck. The reason we have gas masks is because the Germans might drop gas bombs on us, and the masks will stop us from being gassed and dying. We have to take them with us all the time, even when we go to bed.

When our Maureen saw me in mine she started

to cry. Actually, they do look really scary and make you look like a monster ant.

'Why don't you put yours on, our Maureen?' Mum said gently. 'Then you can frighten Nellie!' But our Maureen was so petrified, every time Mum put the mask near her, she screamed blue murder. In the end, Mum put her to bed, and she fell asleep clutching Edna Daffodil and sucking her thumb. The twins thoroughly enjoyed playing monsters with their masks. They chased each other up and down the street with them on shouting, 'I'm the insect man and I'm going to suck your blood!'
It was quite funny watching them really.

Gas masks are actually disgusting things. They stink of rubber and they make your face sweat. We have to take them to school every day and sometimes the teachers pretend there's a German gas attack, and we practise using them. I feel a bit panicky when I first put mine on. It's hard to breathe and they mist up, so when you look out everything looks foggy. But you get used to things when you do them often enough.
    When I say my prayers at night I ask God not to let the Germans drop any gas bombs because I think I might just suffocate in my mask before the gas gets to me.

Our family were going to be evacuated to the country because Neville Chamberlain found out that the Germans planned to drop their first bombs on all our cities. We were in particular danger because, not only did we live in London, which is the capital city of England, but we also live by the docks where our ships are kept, and the Germans will especially want to bomb the docks and destroy our ships.

EVACUATED means that you pack up all your things and leave your house so that you don't get killed when the Germans bomb it. Then you go and live with someone else in the country where it's safer.

Mum, Frank, me, our Maureen, Peter, Paul and baby Daniel were all going to stay in Guildford, while George and Jean were going to stay on at our house. It was like going on holiday! Mum packed all our clothes and made us some food to take for the journey and then we made our way to Paddington train station.

The station was jam packed with people escaping from London. Everywhere was so filled with smoke from the trains that you couldn't see anybody standing on the platforms. You could really hear them though. The noise was so incredibly loud! Everyone was talking at once, and the sound

24

of their voices mixed together and bounced off the ceiling. Our Maureen had her hands over her ears.

Some children were going without their families and they seemed really excited about it.

Frank and the twins were admiring the train engine and watching the engineers stoke the red hot coals in the fire bucket.

'The coals need to be really hot,' Frank was explaining to the twins in a shouting voice, so that they could hear him above the sound of the furiously hissing steam that was coming out of the engine's funnel. 'Then it heats up the water in the boiler above it - a bit like our kettle. That's what makes it go!' He patted the side of the engine lovingly, as if it were a pet dog. 'The engine's called the locomotive.' The twins were beginning to get bored and started to punch each other.

'We need to find somewhere to sit on the train,' Mum said. 'There's a lot of us, so it's going to be difficult to find somewhere with enough room.'
It helped having the pram. Mum just pushed her way through and caught a few people on the ankles with the pram wheels. After that they magically moved out of her way, and somehow she managed to find us a carriage with enough room.

In Guildford we stayed in a large white house
with lots of enormous windows, framed with
beautiful flowery curtains that went all the
way down to the floor. The house belonged to
a doctor and his wife called Dr and Mrs
Jenkins.
Mrs Jenkins loved the baby and she sometimes
looked after him so that Mum could come out
for a walk with us in the countryside. It was
fantastic having her to ourselves for a
while. Dr and Mrs
Jenkins had a big stripy
cat called Tiger. I spent a
lot of time with Tiger. He
spent most of the day
asleep on a cushion on one
of the sitting room sofas
and he seemed to quite
like me. He made a purring
noise like a tiny engine when
I stroked him.
   But we only stayed in
Guildford for two weeks.
One day the twins were
playing German bombers with a load of stones
and broke three of the lovely windows. Dr
Jenkins was really angry. Mrs Jenkins was
really upset. Mum was really embarrassed. The
twins weren't even sorry.
   The Germans hadn't dropped any bombs
anyway, so we went home again. It was a
lovely holiday though. Frank was pleased to

be going back because he didn't want to miss the war. I was a bit sad to be leaving Tiger. I'd never had a pet before.

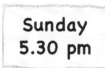

Sunday 5.30 pm

We are listening to the Ovaltiney's children's show on the wireless. It's on at the same time every week. I love it! There's a man called Uncle Johnny who tells stories and jokes, and some children who sing songs, and at the end of the show they give you a secret message in a secret code that you have to decipher. But I never understand what the message is because you need to be a member of the League of Ovaltineys to know the secret code, and I'm not a member. I want to be a member more than anything in the whole world.

My friend, Mary O' Reilly, is a member of the League of Ovaltineys. She has a special League of Ovaltiney's badge and a club book, which she won't show me because it's top secret. She said that I need to buy some Ovaltine (that's a milky drink, in case you didn't know) and when you take the lid off the top there's a little round disc of paper inside that you write your name and address on.

'What you have to do then, Nellie,' she said, 'is to give the paper disc to me and I send it off to the Ovaltineys and tell them all about you, and they'll send you all your own secret club bits.'

I couldn't believe how easy it was. 'That's really good of you, Mary,' I said gratefully.

When I got home I asked Mum about buying some Ovaltine.

'We can't afford it, Nellie,' she said. 'I've got better things to spend my money on.'

'But Mum,' I argued. 'How can I work out the secret code on the Ovaltineys' show unless I'm a member?'

'Can't Mary share hers with you?'

'She's not allowed,' I said shocked, 'It's top secret! I can't believe you said that, Mum!'

Mum wouldn't give in. I'm feeling really grumpy and sulky now. How can I get her to change her mind?

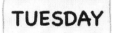 **TUESDAY** Mary came into school today with a new Ovaltiney's comic, which isn't top secret, so she was able to show me. I told her about my conversation with Mum.

'She won't buy any Ovaltine,' I said gloomily. 'I don't know what I'm going to do. I'll never be an Ovaltiney!'
Mary turned the page of her comic and pointed to a message. It said:

> Tell your mothers how
> Ovaltine builds boys and
> girls up if they are
> nervous or poorly, and it
> helps children eat more
> and grow up strong and
> sturdy

'I thought of you, Nell,' she said generously. 'On account of your leg an' all.' She nodded at my knobbly knee.
'I'm sure if your mum thinks it'll make you better she'll get you some.'
I was thrilled. Surely Mum wouldn't be able to resist now!
I spent the rest of playtime copying the message onto a piece of paper so that I wouldn't forget a single word.
 If Mary gets three people to give her their Ovaltine discs she can become a senior member of the League of Ovaltineys. That means she gets a special, real silver-plated badge. She showed me a picture of it. It's

the most brilliant thing I have ever, ever
seen.

'Oh Mary,' I gasped. 'It's just wonderful. Like a piece of treasure or something!' Mary looked quite pleased that I was so enthusiastic.

Mary O'Reilly

'Well, Nellie, you just go and read that message to your mum, and I'm sure you'll soon be a member of our club.'
She said *our* club as if she was in charge of the whole League of Ovaltineys. She swept her arm out grandly as she said it and stuck her nose in the air.
  Mary can be quite annoying and bossy, but I didn't say so because I so badly want to be an Ovaltiney, and I don't want to fall out with her.

  'I've already said no.' I didn't have Mum's full attention, as usual. She was feeding the baby and making the dinner at the same time.
  'Lay the table will you, Nellie?'
  'But Mum, it'll make me grow strong and sturdy, and help me eat more,' I said hopefully.

'You eat me out of house and home as it is,' she replied. 'Eating more is the last thing I want you to do.'

'Mary O' Reilly says it'll be good for my leg.'

'What does Mary O' Reilly know about anybody's legs?' Mum said.

On my way to bed I left the piece of paper on the table, just in case she might read it.

My bed is right under the window and when it's open I can hear Mum talking over the wall to Aunty Dolly, which she does every evening once we're all in bed.

'They say it gives people strength, Dolly, and it might help with her leg,' I could hear her saying. I sat up eagerly and poked my nose out so I could listen.

'I hear they're giving it to our boys in the army, to keep them strong enough to fight the Germans,' Aunty Dolly answered. 'It must be a good thing, Jane.'
They must have been talking about Ovaltine, surely! Fingers crossed, I might be a member of the League of Ovaltineys very soon!

FRIDAY Yippeeeeeee!!!!!!
I got home from school today and Mum had bought some Ovaltine!

31

How to make a lovely cup of
Ovaltine
1. Boil some milk in a saucepan.
2. Add a teaspoon of Ovaltine
   and mix it quickly so that it
   doesn't go lumpy.
3. Drink it!

It's such a lovely brown colour and it tastes
creamy and hot. I sipped it and slurped a
bit.

'Can we have some?' the twins whinged.
'It's not fair if *she* gets it and we don't.'

'It's for my leg,' I told them. 'You don't
have Rickets so you don't need it.'

'I don't mind going without,' our Maureen
smiled angelically. She really is so sweet. I
almost felt guilty that she didn't have any.

Bedtime: I have to share a bed with our
Maureen and Jean. Our Maureen sleeps at one
end of the bed and I'm at the other, so our
feet meet in the middle. We twiddle our toes
together, which makes us giggle. Our
Maureen's toes are always *freezing* cold.
Jean doesn't come to bed until later when
we're fast asleep, so it's like our Maureen
and I have the bed to ourselves. When Jean
does come to bed she takes it in turns to
sleep next to us. I love it when she chooses

32

me. I snuggle up to her and she smells so beautifully of perfume. I rub my neck onto hers so that I can get a bit of the smell. It makes her laugh. 'You're a nutcase, Nellie!' she says.

It's a bit cold at the moment, so we have our coats on the top of the covers to keep us extra warm. They can be a bit itchy so I move them down the bed a bit, but not too far, otherwise my shoulders get cold.

The boys' bed is much more crowded. George and Frank have to share with the twins. I don't envy them that because sometimes Paul wets the bed. Eeerrrkk! George is looking for a flat he can share with some of his friends, and I don't blame him.

Our toilet, which we call the lavvy, is outside in the back yard, but Mum doesn't make us go out there at night as it's so cold and dark, so we widdle in a pot that we keep under the bed. It's not for the other business though. We have to make sure we've done all that before it gets dark, otherwise you have to hold it in and suffer until the morning.

One thing I forgot to say, and it's that Mum has cut out the disc on the Ovaltine tin for me.

'I'll put it up on the high shelf so it's ready for you to take to school,' she said.

The high shelf in the kitchen is Mum's sacred place where she keeps all her important things like our identity cards, which we all have to have, to prove that we are who we say we are and not German spies in disguise. Our ration books are also kept there. The ration books have coupons in them which Mum has to take to the butcher's shop and the clothes' shop to get our food and clothes.

There isn't much in the way of meat and clothes in the shops at the moment because of the war, and the prime minister wants to make sure that everyone gets their fair share. Mum spends a lot of her time standing in the enormously long queue outside the butcher's shop waiting for her meat, because everybody wants meat more than anything else.

SATURDAY I've found my own sacred place where I write my journal. It's behind the armchair that Mum sits in when she feeds the baby. It's a bit dark in there but I can just about see to read. I've told the twins that there's a monster living there who likes to eat little boys, just so they'll leave me alone.

'No, there's not,' said Peter looking a bit uncertain. 'You're a liar, pants on fire.'

'Well, you just go round there and see what happens,' I told him. 'Don't blame me if you get eaten.'

'I will if I like,' he said, poking his tongue out.

But it seems to be working because they haven't yet.

I took the disc into school today to give to Mary O'Reilly.

'How long will it take before I get all my Ovaltiney things?' I asked her.

'I've got to collect discs from two other people first, so it might be a while,' she said vaguely, trying to grab the disc from me, but I held onto it. I wasn't quite ready to let it go.

'Can't I just send off my own one?' I said. 'That way I could send it straight away.' Mary looked really put out. 'You could, Nellie, but I can't get my Senior Membership if you send it off yourself, and that isn't the sort of thing a friend does.'

'Who else is giving you their Ovaltiney discs?' I asked her.

'Well, nobody as yet, but …'

'But I can't wait for ages, Mary, I'm desperate!'

'You won't know where to send it unless I tell you, Nellie!'

'Yes I do, there's an address on the back of the disc.'

'You're such a selfish pig, Nellie Walker!' Mary shrieked, and stormed off across the playground.

Am I? If I give my disc to Mary I could be waiting a whole year if she can't find anybody else. But If I send it off myself I could become a member more quickly and then I could help her recruit some new members - I'm not bothered about a senior membership myself. That sounds like a better plan to me, so I'll write her a note and post it through her letterbox.

Dear Mary,
thank you for introducing me to the League of Ovaltineys.
As you're my very best friend I have decided to recruit some new members for you so that you can get your Silver Membership and that lovely silver badge, just as soon as I get my membership through.

Your friend,
Nellie
xxx

PS. I'm going to bring you in a special present tomorrow.

I haven't actually got a present for Mary.
I'd really like to buy her a gobstopper from
the shop because she loves them. I really
love them too. When you first put them in
your mouth they're so big you can barely suck
them. I like to push them from one cheek to
the other with my tongue, then swallow my
spit, which tastes all sugary sweet. The
more you suck them, the smaller they get, but
they take ages to get smaller so they last a
long time. That's the best thing about them.

Before I can buy the gobstopper there is one
big problem I have to solve:

Problem:
I don't have any money to buy a gobstopper.

Solution
I don't have a solution as yet.

It's no good asking Mum. She hasn't got
any money to spare, so I tried Jean. She was
putting more make-up on at the mirror in the
kitchen.

This is how our conversation went:

'Can you give me a halfpenny, Jean?'

'Why?'

'It's a bit of a secret emergency,' I say mysteriously.

'What sort of secret emergency?'

'If I tell you, you might say no.'

'Try me, you never know. I can't say yes if I don't know what it's for,' she says dabbing powder on her nose.

'Okay then, it's for a gobstopper.'

'No.'

Just *typical*. I wish I'd lied about it. Now there'll probably be a lecture.

'You know that sweets are bad for you, Nellie.'

Off she goes.

Next she'll say they rot my teeth and they'll go all black.

'You know they rot your teeth, and they'll go all black ..." Blah, blah, blah.

'And you'll never get yourself a nice boyfriend …'

I snort scathingly. As if I'd ever want one of those.

I think of an idea.

I might just try telling her the gobstopper's not for me. My teeth won't rot if I'm giving it to someone else, will they? And she won't care about Mary O'Reilly's teeth.

'It's not for me, Jean. It's a present for Mary O'Reilly,' I say looking all angelic and giving.

'Why would you want to give a present to Mary O'Reilly? Is it her birthday or something?'

'Well, no …" I could try telling her about the whole Ovaltiney thing, but actually, I don't think I'll bother. It's obvious Jean isn't going to part with her money.

'Just forget it,' I say and flounce off. She's really into her stride now, going on about not trying to buy friends.

Jean thinking it was Mary O'Reilly's birthday gave me a really good idea. I decided to ask George for the money and tell him it's for a birthday present.

I walked down the road towards the docks when I knew he'd be coming home on his bike. I didn't want Jean to hear our conversation.

Our road looks different since the war started. All the houses have tape criss-crossed onto the windows to stop the glass flying around if a bomb explodes nearby, and there are red buckets filled with sand everywhere, to help put out fires. There are sandbags stacked up outside the butcher's shops. Mum says they're to help protect the walls, and George says they're there to put out any fires. Perhaps it's both. Either way, people feel more secure knowing they are there. The street lamps aren't used anymore at night because of the black-out, and every window in the street is covered with blackout blinds so that no light from the houses can be seen from outside. This is so that when the Germans fly over at night they don't realise that there is a town or city below them because all they can see is black darkness.

But the biggest difference is when you look up. The sky is filled with enormous big, sausage-shaped balloons filled with gas. They're called barrage balloons and they're supposed to stop the Germans bombing the docks. They've got heavy strings on them which are tied to the ground at the dockside. George told me that the German planes are supposed to fly into them and the gas will make the planes explode. Frank hangs around the docks a lot because he wants to be there when it happens.

The other big difference is that we can't play in our local park anymore because it's filled with soldiers and big anti-aircraft guns, and it's got barbed wire all around it, so we just play in the street.

I spotted George and walked into the middle of the road, waving at him just to make sure he saw me. He did and jumped off his bike, smiling at me.

This is my conversation with George:

'What's this, a welcoming committee?'

'George,' I begin … and then I spot double trouble. The twins are making their way towards us. They've got an old pram wheel and they're taking it in turns to push it along with a stick. I need to act quickly.

'I have to get my best friend a birthday present double-quick-fast and I need a halfpenny to get her a gobstopper.' It comes out so fast, I actually say it like this:

'IhavetogetmybestfriendabirthdapresentdoublequickfastandIneedahalfpennytogetheragobstopper.'

George laughs. 'Hey, slow down, Nell. Let me get my brain around that lot!'

'I'll do some errands for you, anything!' I'm pleading now, holding my hands in a praying position. The twins are getting closer. I don't want them to see me taking money from George because they'll go straight to Mum and tell her, and Jean will find out and tell Mum it's not Mary O'Reilly's birthday and that I've been lying to get money from George, and then I'll be in BIG TROUBLE!

'Do you promise to clean my shoes for a month?' George says. George has the most incredibly clean and shiny shoes that he

41

polishes every night until he can see his face in them. I don't know why he bothers because by the time he comes home they're all dirty and dusty again. It's going to take a lot of hard work to get them as clean as he does but I'm desperate.

'Yes, yes,' I promise. 'Anything. *Anything!*'

George is taking a halfpenny out of his pocket and waving it about. I snatch it in an instant and shove it in my pocket … just a smidge before the twins arrive.

'What are you giving our Nellie?' they whinge at George.

'Mind your own business,' I snap at them, and then I'm flying off down the road to the sweetshop before it shuts.

Mary O'Reilly was a bit huffy with me at first, but when she saw the gobstopper her eyes went wide like greedy saucers. She grabbed it out of my hand and rammed it straight into her mouth. 'I forgive you, Nellie,' she tried to say, but the gobstopper made it difficult for her to talk. Some spit dribbled out the side of her mouth.

'Thanks Mary,' I said quickly and turned away. Other people's spit makes me feel a bit queasy.

Mum gave me a stamp, which I earned by doing all the washing-up after dinner, and I sent my disc off to the League of Ovaltineys. Then I cleaned George's shoes, which took me the rest of the evening because George wasn't satisfied with the way I had cleaned them, and I had to keep re-doing them. But all in all, it's been a good day. I'm going to become a member of the Ovaltineys *and* I've managed to keep my best friend!

I did a bit more of my novel:

Desert Hero cont ...

Tex was a man with no money but he had big ideas. He wanted to have his own cattle ranch one day. He worked all day and half the night to save up enough money to make his dreams come true.
He worked in a saloon kitchen doing the washing up, and after that he cleaned people's shoes, but he hadn't saved much because the people he worked for were horrible and greedy, and they didn't pay him enough...

**March 1940
Monday**

When I got home from school there was a letter — an actual letter waiting for me. It was addressed to Miss E Walker.
It was a brown envelope and it was very

thick. It had to be my Ovaltiney membership!
I pressed the envelope all the way round and
turned it over and back again. Then I stroked
it.

 'Aren't you going to open it?' Mum asked.

 'I'm just making the most of it,' I told
her. 'I've never had a letter before.'

 'You're a soppy date,' Mum said smiling.

 I opened it carefully, making sure I didn't
rip the envelope. Inside was the League of
Ovaltineys rule book and on the front cover
it said:

WARNING: Take good care of this book!
It is the official rule book containing the
secrets that only a member of the League
of Ovaltineys may know. These secrets
are strictly private – only for the eyes of
 members, and their parents, who are
considered as honorary members …
If it should be accidentally lost, anyone
who finds it should return it at once,
without reading, to the owner, whose
name is on the back cover.

I could hardly breathe, it was so exciting.
I went into my special place behind the
chair, made myself comfortable and turned the
first page. There was a picture of the
Ovaltineys' membership badge.

And underneath it said:

> To obtain yours all you have to do is to
> complete the form sent with this book

I was a bit disappointed — I thought I was
going to get the badge straight away. That
would mean another stamp and another long
wait! I had a last feel in the envelope just
in case they'd put one in by mistake, but it
wasn't there.

Still, there was plenty of reading to do,
and as I turned over the pages I realised how
lucky I was to be part of a secret club.
There were secret passwords, signs and
signals to do with other Ovaltineys. And the
SECRET CODE! I've also decided to copy it
into the back of my journal just in case
something nasty happens to my rule book.

A = 2. B = 4 C = 6. D = 8. E = 10. F = 12. G = 14. H = 16.
I = 18. J = 20. K = 22. L = 24. M = 26. N = 28. O = 30. P = 32.
Q = 34. R = 36. S = 38. T = 40. U = 42. V = 44. W = 46.
X = 48. Y = 50. Z = 52

I've written my very first message in
Ovaltiney code:

16 10 24 24 30   10 44 10 36 50 30 28 10

....

If you don't want to work out the code, I've
written all the messages in the back of my
journal.

This is message No. 1

Now to find
somewhere really
safe to hide my rule
book.

I can't even think of a number 3 because there is absolutely nowhere in this house that I can call my own. I share a bedroom, I share a bed, I share absolutely everything. **I HAVE NO PRIVACY!!!** Everwhere here is so crowded that there's hardly enough air to breathe.

Mum came in. 'Are you behind that chair again, Nellie?' she said. The twins were behind her, peering in at me. Peter had his finger up his nose searching for something nasty.

'Why don't you sit on the chair like normal people?' Paul shouted at me.

'I'm trying to get away from twerps like you,' I shouted back at him.

'All right, Nellie,' Mum said. 'There's no need for name calling.'

'What've you got there, Nellie?' Peter had slid under the chair and grabbed my envelope. I kicked out at him and shouted, 'Mum, get them away will you? Why can't I have any privacy? Is it too much to ask?'

'Go and get your tea from the table, you two,' Mum told them. They went off muttering, trying to kick each other in the shins.

'Hello Nellie, can I come in with you?' That was our Maureen. She pushed her head in next to mine. 'Ooh, it's a bit dark in here. Aren't you frightened sitting in here by yourself?'

'Clear off Maureen, this is my space.'

'Nellie, I told you about being rude just now.' Mum's voice was cross. 'Come out and have your tea, and you as well Maureen. Peter, wash your hands before you touch that bread, there's something horrible on your finger. Paul, stop prodding the baby, you'll wake him up.'

'Waaaaahhhhhhhhh!' screamed the baby. I felt like I was suffocating, like I do when I have my gas mask on. I grabbed my things and ran out into the yard and I just stood still, breathing big gulps of air and looking up at the small piece of sky I could see in between the tall buildings.

Then I thought of the ideal place to read my rule book. There, in front of me, was the lavvy - empty for once. I went in, shut the door and sat on the seat. Peace at last!

**TUESDAY** I did the Ovaltiney 'Secret High Sign' to Mary O'Reilly today. You put the fingers of your right hand into an 'O' shape. It's what you do to say hello to other members of the League of Ovaltineys. She did the same back to me. Then she said, 'Give the password.' And I said, 'Ovaltiney – Ovaltiney.' I said it very quietly so that the other children in the playground didn't hear what I was saying.

'What are you two whispering about?' Joyce Wallace said. Joyce's a girl in our class. She only looks about six because she's quite small, but also she's really silly and only ever wants to play fairies. She usually plays with the younger children.

'Just our secret club code,' I told her.

'Can I join?' she asked. I looked at Mary and she looked back at me, shaking her head. Joyce just isn't League of Ovaltineys material.

Evening: I have a hiding place for my journal and Ovaltiney rule book now but I've had to tell Mum. She's allowing me to keep them on her high shelf. I had to swear her to secrecy and make her promise not to read my journal.

'Cross your heart, hope to die, stick a needle in your eye,' I said.

'Cross my heart, hope to die, stick a needle in my eye,' Mum repeated solemnly.

I had to do the washing up again after dinner today to earn another stamp for my badge. Then I had to clean George's shoes. I don't have much time in the evenings to play or write my journal at the moment, but at least I've sent off for the badge.

Almost a whole month later!

I HAVE TWO LOTS OF GOOD NEWS:

No 1. A second letter arrived for me today. It was my Ovaltiney badge – finally! I pinned it to my dress, on the left-hand side of my chest.

'I think yours is slightly smaller than mine,' Mary smirked nastily when I showed it to her at school. 'That's a shame for you, Nellie. It's probably something to do with the war, and the Ovaltineys not being able to use so much metal or something.'

I looked at them both. They looked exactly the same to me.

'Take yours off, Mary, and we'll compare them,' I said. But she wouldn't.

She's so annoying, she always has to think she's better than me!

No 2. I have finally finished my month of slavery, and no longer have to clean George's shoes. I never want to look at shoe polish again and I vow never, ever to clean another shoe. I will let my own shoes get mucky and even muckier and I don't care.

May 1940
Monday

Our church is always busy at Easter and our school takes part in the church WHITSUNDAY PROCESSION every year. A procession is a lot of people walking slowly through the streets dressed up in smart clothes, and marching bands playing marching music. Our church has a statue called the Sacred Heart, which is actually a statue of Jesus with his heart showing outside of his clothes. The heart is painted red so that you can see it easily and it's supposed to show that He cares about everyone. The statue is going to be decorated with flowers and carried through the streets as if it is really Jesus himself.

Each year one boy and one girl is chosen by our local priest, Father Joseph, to carry the school banner. It's a real honour to be chosen, but as yet I never have been. Mary O'Reilly's been chosen three times. She always has a lovely new white dress to wear. I usually have to stand near the back as I don't look particularly special, apart from the blue velvet ribbon in my hair.

'I'm having another new, white dress,' Mary O'Reilly told me at playtime. 'With a silk ribbon round the waist.'

'It sounds lovely, Mary,' I said enthusiastically.

'I don't suppose you'll be having anything new, Nellie, will you?' she looked at me pityingly.

'I don't know,' I said, feeling myself going a bit red. 'I hadn't thought about it much.' Which was actually a fib because, truthfully, I was desperate to look as pretty as Mary.

I told Frank about it on the way home from school.

'I don't know why you go round with her,' Frank frowned. 'She's just a big snob. She's not a real friend to you. All she does is boast to you and you're stupid enough to take it all in.'

'Oh no,' I told him. 'She really likes me and I'm really lucky to be her best friend. She's so pretty and popular.'

We're doing procession rehearsals tomorrow and Father Joseph is coming to the school to announce who the banner holders are. Everyone is really excited.

WEDNESDAY When I got to school Mary O'Reilly was looking very confident and pleased with herself. For some reason, I feel really irritated with her. I never expected to be chosen when I was wearing my callipers, but now that my legs aren't so ugly, surely I must be in with a chance?

After playtime we went into the assembly hall and Father Joseph was already on the stage, smiling at everyone.

'Good morning children,' he said, once we all settled down and stopped talking.

'Good mor-ning Fa-ther Jo-seph,' we all chanted together.

'This year I've had some help with choosing the banner carriers.' He pointed to Miss Robinson, who stepped forward. 'And we have decided to choose two children who have worked really hard in school all year and deserve to have a special treat.' Everyone turned to each other all excited and began whispering.

'Miss Robinson will announce the winners,' Father Joseph said.

Miss Robinson stepped forward and cleared her throat. 'The two children are …'

My heart was thumping and I didn't look at anyone. I was praying in my head, 'please let her choose me, please let it be me …'

'David Holland!' There was a cheer as David got a delighted thump on the back from his friends.

'And now for the girls …'

'Please choose me, please choose me …'

'Nellie Walker!'

There was complete silence in the hall. It took a second for me to realise that my name had been called. Mary was staring at me as if she couldn't believe it. Her mouth was opening and closing like a fish. Nobody thumped me on the back and congratulated me. Then I heard somebody whisper,

'But she can't walk properly, and her face is always dirty.'

I found myself rubbing my face with the back of my hand. No dirt came off.

Then Father Joseph was talking. 'Can both children stand up and we'll give them a "well done" round of applause.' David and I stood up. Miss Robinson was beaming at me. I smiled back, shyly. Everybody clapped politely except Mary O'Reilly. She was trying not to cry.

Mum was so excited that I'd been chosen.

'You're the first one in our family that's ever carried the banner, Nellie,' she said. 'It's such an honour!'

Jean gave me a big hug when she came in.

'I'll do your hair for you on the day,' she said.

'Thanks Jean,' I said gratefully. It was nice being the centre of attention.

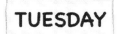 **TUESDAY** When I got home Mum was looking very pleased with herself. 'I've got a surprise for you, Nellie,' she said. 'I've managed to get something beautiful for you to wear for the procession.'
I was so excited I could hardly wait. Lying on a chair was a white lacy dress. But as I looked closer, I didn't feel as excited anymore. It wasn't new, but I wasn't expecting a new dress anyway. It wasn't the fact that it was far too big either, or that it was so old-fashioned. It was the big yellow stain the size of a dinner plate in the middle of the chest that really worried me.
'One of my customers gave it to me for you.' she said. 'I know it's a bit big, but it's really good quality. I can take it up a bit for you, and I'll be able to get the stain out, I'm sure.'
I tried to keep smiling but I was finding it really difficult. 'How will you find the time Mum?' I said. 'You're always so busy.'
'Don't you worry about that,' she said. 'I can always find time for my girl.'
I looked at her hands, all red and dry and cracking from doing other people's washing, and I felt really guilty.

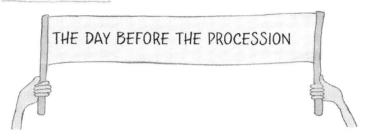

THE DAY BEFORE THE PROCESSION

Mary's been a bit strange with me since I was chosen to carry the banner. When anybody else is around she pretends to be nice to me. But when there's nobody about she ignores me. So I was quite surprised when she invited me round to her house today.

'I want your opinion about my dress for the procession,' she said.

'Of course, Mary,' I said straight away, really relieved that she was being normal with me again.

'You wait in the parlour while I put it on, and then I'll come in wearing it,' she said. I'd never been in her parlour before. It's a lovely room with a fireplace and two comfy chairs. There's a table by the window with a pretty white tablecloth over it. We don't have a parlour - just a fireplace with the one chair that I hide behind.

Mary came back in and I couldn't help gasping. The dress was *beautiful*. The white skirt was all lacy and sticking out with

56

pearls and roses on it. She looked like a
princess. She even had a purple velvet cloak
to wear over the top. And she hadn't even
been picked to carry anything special like I
had.
I touched the cloak and it felt really warm
and silky smooth. I wanted one so badly I
felt sick.

'My mum says I should have been picked to
carry the banner instead of you,' Mary said
twirling around to show me the back, 'Because
I'm prettier than you, and your dress will be
second-hand and not nearly as nice as mine
because your mum's so poor.'

I felt confused. Mary was talking to me in
a nice voice, and she'd invited me into her
parlour as if she was still my friend, but
what she was saying to me was really cruel
and horrible. And worse still, she was being
unkind about my mum.

I felt a big lump in my throat. I know
we're not as well-off as some people, but Mum
works so hard, and she does her best. She
just has so many children to feed.

Then something inside me became hot and
angry. I felt my mouth opening and these
words poured out as if they had a mind of
their own:

'You're just a big, nasty show-off, Mary
O'Reilly,' the words said as I ran to the
front door. 'And by the way, you look really

fat in your dress. It makes your big bum look even more enormous!'

I wish I could have laughed at the shocked look on her face but I was too upset. I cried all the way home.

Mum wasn't there when I got in. She'd gone to the shops. George was home from work and was having a cup of tea. My finished dress was draped over the chair ready for me to try on.

'Aha!' he cried, bowing before me as if I were royalty. 'Here comes the chosen one!' He stopped smiling when he saw my face. 'What's up, mate?'

'I don't want to talk about it,' I said. He saw me looking at the dress.

'What's this monstrosity?' he said picking it up.

Mum had done her best, but it looked even worse, if that was possible. Because the dress was now smaller, the stain looked even bigger. She hadn't managed to get it out. I tried the dress on. The neck was too big and it stuck out under my chin. It was longer at the front than it was at the back. George began to laugh.

'You look really dreadful!'

I started crying again. George stopped laughing.

'Aaw! Don't cry Nell, I didn't mean it!'

At that moment Jean came in. 'Good grief! That looks hideous!' she shrieked.

'Poor old Nellie can't wear this tomorrow to the procession, Jean,' said George. 'Our family will be a laughing stock.' He put his hand in his pocket and handed some money to her.

'I've just been paid,' he said. 'Take Nellie to the shops and buy her a new one. You can add some money to it as well.'

'I'll probably need to use all of our clothing coupons,' Jean replied reaching up to the high shelf. 'Come on, Nellie. We can catch the next bus if we're really quick.'

We bought the most beautiful dress I have ever, ever seen. I swirled round and round in it like I never wanted to stop. The skirt floated through the air around me as if it were a dancing cloud.

'I'm not just a princess,' I breathed. 'I'm better than that. I'm a fairy princess!'

It's ten times better than Mary O'Reilly's.

I can't wait until tomorrow!

THE DAY OF THE PROCESSION

Miss Robinson smiled enormously when she saw me in my dress. 'Well, look at you, Nellie Walker,' she said. 'The King himself would mistake you for one of his daughters if he saw you!'

Jean had put rags in my hair the night before, and sprayed sugar water on my curls in the morning to keep them in place, but they had mostly fallen out by the time I got to the church. I didn't care though. I felt wonderful because of what Miss Robinson had said to me.

I carried the banner with Dave Holland all the way round the streets without dropping it, even though my arms ached like anything. I could see Mum waving madly in the crowd with George and Jean.

I couldn't concentrate on the church service, I was too busy feeling the lacy material of my dress. I must have smoothed it over my knees a thousand times. Mary O'Reilly looked at me twice in a nasty way but I pretended not to notice her. After church we went to the church hall and had tea and cakes. I ate four jam tarts.

Everyone was admiring my dress and saying how beautiful I looked and how well I had carried the banner. It was the best day of my life — by far!

MONDAY I said goodbye to my lovely dress today. Jean took it to the pawnshop and sold it to them, then she and George split the money between them. Of course I couldn't keep it, what would be the point? I'd never wear it again.

In case you're really rich and you haven't had to find out what a PAWN SHOP is, it's a shop that buys things from you, and then when you've got enough money you can buy them back again. Mum takes our winter coats there when the weather gets warmer, and then she saves up the money to get them back in the Autumn.

Sometimes the people that she works for give us their children's old coats. Then Mum doesn't need to buy back our old ones and she can use the money for other things like food.

I played by myself at playtime this week and Mary O'Reilly played with Kathleen Doyle. I didn't care. I took my book outside and wrote a bit more of my Johnny Mack Brown story. I haven't done any for a while.

I still had to sit next to Mary in the classroom because we'd always sat together and you aren't allowed to move about. She moved herself in her chair so that her back was facing me. It saved me the bother of having to turn my back on her.

Desert Hero cont ...

Tex was a loner. He had no home or family or friends, apart from his faithful horse, Silver Mist.
 He roamed from town to town doing brave deeds, but no one got to know him well. He didn't need any friends ...

WEDNESDAY

We had another evacuation rehearsal at school today. All the children and teachers have to walk to the train station with their gas masks round their necks as if we were really getting on the train. We have to walk in pairs along the pavement, which is called walking in a CROCODILE. We didn't make much of a crocodile this time because a lot of children from our school were still in the country from last time we were evacuated.

We had to line up in groups on the platform as if we were waiting to get on a train. I had to stand with Frank, Maureen and the twins as we're from the same family.

'This is boring,' Paul moaned. 'Why do we have to do all this? The Germans aren't even dropping bombs on us.'

Even though he badly gets on my nerves, I have to agree with him.

Every so often the sirens sound, to warn us that German bombers might be coming, and we all rush to the air-raid shelter. Actually, that's not strictly true. We *used* to rush when it all started, but now we just dawdle. There's no hurry because it's just a practice. Some people don't even bother going to the air-raid shelters anymore. They just sit under the table in their houses. Aunty Dolly next door sits in her armchair and puts her feet up. 'If they're coming for me, I'll die in comfort,' she says.

After a while the ALL CLEAR sounds and we charge out hoping to see lots of fire and bombed buildings, but we're always disappointed. The Germans still haven't come and the houses are still in one piece.

**June 1940
Saturday**

There was a new Johnny Mack Brown film on at the penny pictures this morning. I went with Frank and his mates as I'm still not speaking to Mary O'Reilly. Frank wasn't very happy about it, but Mum said she wouldn't give him the money if he didn't take me.

'Aren't there any other girls you can make friends with?' he moaned.

I've given it a great deal of thought. There aren't so many children in our class now. There's Kathleen Doyle, but Mary O'Reilly's grabbed her. All the other girls are best friends with each other apart from Joyce Wallace. There's no way I want to play fairies with Joyce Wallace.

Desert Hero continued ...

Tex thought it was time to move on. He saddled up Silver Mist and they travelled for three days before they came to another town which was called Ridgeway Creek. It seemed deserted, even though it was the afternoon.

Tex found a saloon bar and went inside.

"I'll have a cup of tea," he said to the bartender.

WEDNESDAY On our way home from school we walk past a row of big, posh houses with white steps leading up to shiny, black front doors. There's a girl who lives there, but she doesn't go to my school because she's Jewish and she goes to a separate Jewish school. She has long, black hair which she usually wears in two plaits. Although I've never spoken to her, I feel as if I know her

65

because my mum does her family's washing. Her name's Sarah and she's a few months older than me. Mum says she's very clever and her family expect her to be a doctor one day. She's usually playing by herself on her steps when we go by.

I don't take much notice of her normally because I'm too busy chatting to Mary. But I noticed her today for two reasons:

1. I wasn't walking home with Mary, just our Maureen and the twins, and I wasn't too busy having a conversation.

2. Sarah was sitting on her middle step reading a book. It's quite unusual for anybody to be outside reading a book where I live. Even on the inside for that matter. I'm actually the only other person I know who reads without being forced to.

As we passed her, she looked up at me and smiled. I found myself smiling back. I felt a bit shy that she had noticed me.

'Hello Nellie,' she said. She knew my name!

'Hello Sarah,' I said back. 'What are you reading?'

'Little Women,' she said. 'By Louisa May Allcott. Have you heard of it?'

'I've read it,' I told her.

66

She looked surprised. I understood why because of reason two that I just wrote about. 'I borrowed it from the library; I often go there.'

Suddenly, for a change, I wanted Sarah to know that I was different from everybody else. Usually I get teased for being different. The main reason is my legs, but I also get teased for being a teacher's pet and a SWOT, which is an insulting name for someone who likes learning things. I got the feeling though, that Sarah would approve of me being different. She seemed different too.

'I go to the library too,' she said. 'I love reading.'

'Who's your favourite character?' I asked.

'I haven't made up my mind yet, I've only read a little bit.'

'I like Jo. She wants to be a writer – like I do.'

Sarah looked surprised again. I felt quite proud that I was writing a novel. I was just wondering if I should start to tell her about it, when Peter started to whinge, 'Come on Nellie, hurry up. We want to go home!'

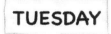 I had an embarrassing moment in school today. Our Maureen came up to me at playtime and asked me if I wanted to play with her and her

67

friends. Honestly, I could have died of shame! Mary and Kathleen Doyle were watching.

'Clear off Maureen!' I hissed.

'But you're all by yourself,' she said. 'I don't like to see you without a friend.'
I heard someone snigger.

'Clear off, will you?' I said again. I stomped off so that I couldn't see the hurt tears in her eyes. I know she was just being kind and lovely, but I felt like slapping her.

I'll have to bring something to do during playtime tomorrow so that I look too busy to worry about friends. I know! I'll bring my notebook and write some more of my novel.

Desert Hero continued ...

There was a girl sitting in the corner who smiled at him. Although Tex never usually bothered to make friends, he went over to sit with her.

"I'm Tex, pleased to meet you," he said.

"I'm Bella," she replied. She had a cowboy hat on and two dark plaits hanging down her back. She had a cup of tea as well ...

THURSDAY

Challenge for the Day
I'm going to smile for as
long as I can

It's actually much harder than you would think. After a few minutes my jaw was aching and people were looking at me in a funny way.

'Why do you keep smiling?' Jean asked me. She was sitting in the chair, sewing up a hole in her stocking.

'I'm trying to make myself happy,' I told her, trying to push past her and into my secret place.

'Why don't you go outside and get out from under my feet?' she grumbled. 'That would make me happy.

I gave her my biggest, brightest smile, but I meant it in a sarcastic way.

FRIDAY

Jean came home today after work with a dark green uniform in her arms.

'Guess what?' she said. 'I've joined the WVS!'

That stands for the WOMEN'S VOLUNTARY SERVICE. She'll make tea for people if they get bombed out by the Germans. She's also hoping to learn how to drive an ambulance so that she can take casualties to hospital.

I felt a bit sad that she wouldn't be working at the dress shop anymore. They always gave her such nice clothes to wear.

'Oh no, Nellie, I've still got to work there,' she said. 'I do the WVS after work. We all have to do our bit for the war effort, you know.'

'We'll hardly see anything of you,' Mum sniffed. But I think she was quite proud of Jean really, and Jean looked lovely in her uniform. It's very exciting that somebody in our family is going to learn to drive an actual ambulance.

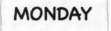

MONDAY

I saw Sarah on the step outside her house again today, She'd read a bit more of "Little Women".

'I think I like Jo too,' she said. 'It's made me think that I might start writing a novel, just like you, Nellie.'

I was really pleased that somebody as clever as Sarah wanted to do something that I was doing. I went a bit pink on my cheeks.

70

I spoke to Mum about it when I got home from school. She had made us some bread and dripping, which I love. I sit and lick the fatty bits off first and then I nibble all the crust round the outside. Then I finally eat the soft bit in the middle.

'I think she's trying to make friends with you, Nellie.' Mum said. 'Why don't you ask her to play with you?'

'But what if she doesn't want to?' I said. 'I'd feel really stupid then.'

Frank laughed, spitting a bit of his bread on the table. 'You're daft, you are Nellie!' he said.

'Manners, Frank,' Mum said. She smiled at me. 'Sometimes Nellie, you just have to be a bit brave and do things you're not quite sure about. After all, what's the worst that can happen?'

'A big bomb could drop on them both! BOOM!! BOOM!!' Peter shouted.

'Yeah!' agreed Paul. 'And their stupid books would burst into flames and set the whole world alight!' The twins thought this was hilarious and ran around the house pretending to be aeroplanes dropping bombs. Maureen looked frightened.

'Outside and play, you two,' Mum ordered. 'You'll wake the baby, and I've only just got him to sleep.'

Mum made Frank take our Maureen and the twins home today so that I could talk to Sarah without constantly being interrupted by two annoying little twits.

I had my novel in my school satchel and I showed it to her. She read it very carefully and then handed it back to me.

'I think it's really exciting, Nellie,' she said. 'Where do you get your ideas from?'

'Mostly from the flicks on a Saturday morning.'

'The flicks?'

'Yes, you know, the picture house, the Troxy. They show all the best films. Don't you ever go there?'

Sarah shook her head. 'No, I don't. It's the Sabbath on a Saturday - our day of rest and prayer.' Sarah explained. 'It's like you going to church on Sundays.'

'That's a real shame, Sarah,' I said. 'You're missing out on so many great Westerns.'

Desert Hero continued ...

Tex and Bella had a long conversation
while they were drinking their tea.
They found they both liked horses and
they both wanted to own a cattle ranch
one day. Tex felt good. He'd never had
a real friend before.

WEDNESDAY I walked past Sarah's house
again today. She was sitting
on her step, writing in an exercise book.
She jumped up when she saw me.
   'I've started writing a journal, Nellie,'
she said. 'And on the very first page I
decided to write about meeting you.'
I was so thrilled! I was starring in someone
else's life story!
   I was a bit late home because I had spent
so long with Sarah, but when I explained to
Mum she didn't mind.

FRIDAY

Morning: Sarah's school is further away than
mine so she cycles every day. She's asked me
if I could meet her on the way home from
school today and Mum has said it's all right
but I've got to take the twins along with me

73

again. Luckily, our Maureen's staying home
today with a stinking cold.

Afternoon: I had to take a slightly different
route and it took me a bit longer. After a
while I saw Sarah riding her bike and waved
so that she would see me and not ride past.
She jumped off and walked along beside me.
Peter and Paul lagged behind us. 'Why do we
have to go this way, Nellie?' Paul whined.
'It's taking ages!'

'You don't have to walk with us,'
I told him. 'Go home by
yourselves and stop pestering
us.'

'But Mum says we're not
to, we have to stay with
you,' Peter
looked
cross.
I sighed.
I don't
know why I
have to
look after
them when Frank is just
allowed to go off with his mates,
and he's older than me.
'All right, stay with us then,' I said.
'But keep your traps shut. I'm trying to have
a conversation.'

We were so busy talking, we'd reached
Sarah's house before we realised it.

'Can you come out and play for a bit?' I
asked her.
She shook her head, 'Not tonight, Nellie,'
she told me. 'It's the Sabbath again.'
I must have looked a bit disappointed because
she said that she would play out on Monday
after school.

SATURDAY Although we go to church on
Sunday mornings, I still have
to go to CONFESSION in our
church on Saturdays before we go to the
pictures.

It's really annoying. We have to go one by
one into a little box room inside the church
and shut the door. Then you have to kneel
down and you face a metal grid in the wall
while a priest sits in another little box on
the other side of the grid. You're not
supposed to know who's there, but Father
Joseph has a wheezy chest, so you can always
tell when it's him.
He starts off by saying, 'What is your
confession, my child?'

This is the bit that I find quite tricky.
You're supposed to tell him all the naughty
things you've done during the week. The
trouble is, I can't always think of much
that I've done wrong. I don't mean to be
boastful or anything, but I don't make a

habit of doing really awful things like robbing banks or murdering people; I think I'm pretty good normally. So I just usually say, 'I've been lying to my mother again, Father, and I stole a biscuit from our biscuit tin.'

We haven't really got a biscuit tin; we never have any biscuits in our house, so that's actually a lie, but Father Joseph just nods and he seems quite satisfied with that.

'Say three Hail Mary's and God will forgive you,' he says. "Hail Mary" is a prayer that we learnt in school, and it's quite a short prayer so I'm happy to do that if it means my not really-real sins are forgiven.

They were showing the same Johnny Mack Brown film again this week at the pictures. I really enjoyed seeing it for a second time. It was called BORN TO THE WEST. Johnny played the part of a man called Tom who owned a cattle ranch. John Wayne was also in it, and he played a man who lost all his money and his cattle at the card table, and Tom helped him get them back. It's given me some more great ideas for my novel.

Before the film starts they always show a little film about what's going on in the war. Today they showed one about our Spitfire pilots shooting down lots of German Messerschmitt planes. Even though the Germans have lots more planes than us, our

pilots are so skilful and brave, they manage
to shoot most of the Germans down. You
should see the German planes trying to make a
run for it!

MONDAY

Sarah and I played marbles for a while
outside her house after school. The twins
found some snails and tried to race them.
Our Maureen sat on Sarah's step and played
with a stick. Mum says that she's going to
make Frank take his turn walking the young
ones home from school so that I can play with
Sarah more often.

THURSDAY I play with Sarah quite a lot
after school now. I take our
Maureen with me because she's
found that one of the girls in her class
lives across the road from Sarah, so they
play mums and dads together.

Sometimes I go inside Sarah's house. I was a
bit nervous the first time I went in, but her
Mum is really nice. Sarah's dad owns a
tailor's shop and used to make men's suits,
but Sarah says he's now making soldiers'
uniforms and is really busy all the time.
Sarah's mum is called Mrs Cohen. She has

dark hair like Sarah and she wears it in
waves, a bit like Jean. She has lipstick on
as well, and her clothes are really
beautiful. I was quite surprised - I didn't
know mums dressed like that. My mum always
has a pinafore on so that she doesn't spoil
her dress, and she wears her hair in a bun.
She never, ever wears lipstick.

Sarah's house is enormous compared to ours.
She has a front parlour that they only use
for best. It's a bit like Mary O'Reilly's,
but bigger and posher. Sarah opened the door
a bit to show me once. It was full of
gorgeous chairs and cabinets with beautiful
china in it, and the fireplace had a lovely
golden mirror above it. There was a
patterned rug with red roses on, in front of
the fire. It was so lovely.
  We only live in the bottom part of our
house. Joe and Kathleen Walsh live at the top
of our stairs. They were married last year
and Kathleen is having a baby soon. Our
family all sleep downstairs in what should be
the front parlour. You can't see any floor
in the room because it's covered in beds
pushed together at all different angles. We
don't use the fireplace because the boys' bed
is pushed up against it.
  Sarah has her own bedroom upstairs, and her
two older brothers sleep in yet another one.
Being in Sarah's house is like living in a

different world, although it's only four
streets away from mine.

Miss Robinson has noticed that
I'm writing my novel at
playtime and asked if she
might have a read of it. I gave it to her at
the end of playtime and said I needed it back
by the next playtime. I didn't want her to
realise that I had nobody to play with.

   She gave it back to me in time and said
that I might want to make the other
characters more *real* to the reader and give
them more to say. I've decided to call the
bartender DAVE.

Desert Hero cont ...

There was going to be a card game at the saloon,
where all the players had to put their own money
on the table, and the winner won all of the money.
Tex didn't usually play card games but he was
thinking of playing because he was too poor to
buy his cattle ranch.

   "But you might lose all your money," Bella
exclaimed. "And then it would take you years
to save again!"

   "It's a chance I'm going to have
to take," Tex said. "Count me in!"
he shouted to Dave the bartender.
"And I'll have another cup of
tea, while you're there!"

79

We finished school today for the summer. Miss Robinson said that she was going to stay with her mum and sister in Lewisham. Before she went she gave me some more exercise books.

'Make sure you keep writing, Nellie,' she told me. 'Remember, an author writes every day, even if it's only a little bit.'

'But I can't always think of things to write,' I told her.

'I know it can be hard, but you have to get into the habit of doing it,' she replied. 'You've got a real talent and it's important that you use it.'

I hadn't intended to do much writing in the holidays because I planned to do a lot of playing with Sarah. We're best friends now, and she is a much better friend than Mary O'Reilly ever was. We play all sorts of games and she's promised to teach me how to ride her bicycle.

She's got lots of things, just like Mary, but she doesn't show off about them, she really likes to share everything. She even gave our Maureen a doll, and Mrs Cohen gave my mum some lovely clothes for our Maureen that Sarah had grown out of. Mum was ever so pleased.

'These are really good quality, Nellie,' she said holding up a yellow smock dress. 'Our Maureen will look like a little sweetheart in this.'

It's so hot I can hardly be bothered to do anything. Sarah and I went to play down by the docks because we thought it would be cooler near the water, but the soldiers told us to clear off. We went back to my street and played Gobs instead.

How to play GOBS (or five stones)

You need five small stones plus another one to be the ball. It's a good idea to have a smooth stone for the ball.

1. Put five stones in a group.
2. Throw the ball in the air (not too high.)
3. While the ball's in the air pick up the five stones and scatter them on the ground. (Not too far away from each other.)

4. Catch the ball in the same hand.
5. Throw the ball up again. This time while it's in the air, pick up a stone 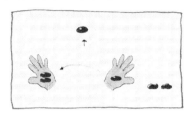 with the same hand and put it into your other hand.
6. Catch the ball in the same hand.
7. Repeat until you have all five stones in your other hand. Then you have won!
8. If you drop the ball it's the other person's turn.

September 7th 1940
Saturday

I'm writing this in our air-raid shelter. A little while ago we were playing outside as usual, when the warning siren went off.

'Come on everyone,' Mum said. 'Let's get going.'
We all groaned.

'Do we have to?' Frank said. 'The Germans aren't going to come.'

'Can't I go and sit with Aunty Dolly?' I
asked. But Mum, as ever, insisted that we
get our gas masks and go over to the air-raid
shelter. It's in one of the wharves by the
dock. A wharf is a big warehouse that stores
the goods that the ships bring into the
docks. I grabbed my journal and put it in
with my gas mask.

But this time it's different. We're sitting
here in the dark and we can hear explosions
outside. The ground is shaking and the
explosions are getting closer. Mum is
staying cheerful like the other grown-ups,
but it's quite scary.
  Our Maureen keeps crying and so does the
baby, so I offered to give our Maureen a
cuddle. She's got her thumb in her mouth and
she's hiding her head under my armpit.
  The twins are playing bombers again and
keep tripping over people's legs. The place
is full to bursting with people. I can't see
Sarah. I hope she's here somewhere.

We stayed in the air raid shelter for hours,
but eventually the ALL CLEAR siren sounded
and we came out. It was hard to believe what
we were seeing. The whole docks were alight,
the sky was red with flames and the air
around us was black with smoke. There was a
terrible smell of burning. The streets were
crowded with people coming out of the

shelters and it was difficult to try and stay together. Lots of people began to cry because their houses had gone and in their place were just piles of bricks. Some houses were on fire, with flames lashing through holes where the windows had been. Fire engine bells were going off and firemen were pointing gushing hoses at the buildings. I held our Maureen's hand tightly. Frank had the twins and Mum had the baby.

Luckily our house was still standing. The bombs seemed to have missed our street. 'Let's get that kettle on,' Mum said cheerfully. There was a queue for the lavvy because they didn't have one in the air raid shelter and everyone was busting for a wee.

Mum made us all a cup of tea and we had some bread and dripping.
   'Do you think Jean and George are all right, Mum?' Frank said.
   'Of course they are, Frank,' she nodded. 'Jean's going to be a bit busy tonight helping people, so I don't suppose we'll see her for a bit. I think the best thing to do is for us all to get some sleep and things will look better in the morning.'
   'I don't want to go to sleep,' Peter moaned. 'I want to go out and watch the houses burning!'
   'So do I!' Paul joined in.

Our Maureen started crying. 'Where's George?' she snivved, and the noise set the baby off.

'Don't worry, Our Maureen. I expect he's safe in another shelter,' Frank said.'He'll be back soon.' Then he began to yawn widely and stretch his arms above his head. 'I'm really tired, aren't you, Nellie?' He nodded at me in an exaggerated way. I thought he was being daft at first, but then I realised he was trying to get the boys to bed so that Mum could have some peace. He seemed really grown up then. I nodded and I did an enormous, dramatic yawn as well. 'Come on, our Maureen, I think it's time we went to bed.'

Mum looked at us both gratefully. 'I'll come in to you in a bit. Don't worry about a wash tonight, just get straight into your night things.'

Peter and Paul stopped moaning at the thought of getting away with not washing, and Frank managed to get them to sleep, but not before they'd had a jumping session on the bed, pretending to be firemen and making whooshing noises like water coming from a hosepipe.

I just snuggled down with our Maureen and put my arm around her. She soon went to sleep.

Desert Hero cont ...

They were in the middle of the card game when the saloon door burst open and a gang of baddies burst in, led by Mad Man McBlaine

"Who left me out of the game?" he shouted. The baddies reached for their guns and started firing. Tex grabbed his money and dived under a table. He was there for what seemed like forever, his heart beating like a drum, bang, bang, bang, it went. Bang, bang, bang, went the shots.

Then, suddenly they stopped...

SUNDAY

We're back in the air raid shelter and the bombs are dropping again. I feel more scared than I did yesterday. I know they said on the wireless that bombs would be dropped one day. It took so long for it to happen that we almost wanted it to because it seemed really exciting, but now it's happened and I've seen the damage that bombs do, there's nothing exciting about it.

George got home shortly after we did. He had a cup of tea with Mum and then went to bed. I woke up early this morning, as Jean got into our bed. She'd been up all night helping people who were hurt in the bombing.

86

Mum was sitting in the chair dressed in the same clothes she'd had on last night. I don't think she'd been to bed at all. She chucked us all out of the house so that Jean could get some sleep.

I took our Maureen and the twins for a wander round to see what was happening. The road next to ours had taken some hits. Three of the houses had been bombed and the people who lived there were picking over the bricks, looking for their things. I decided to go to Sarah's house to see if she was all right.

When I got there I couldn't believe what I saw. Sarah's lovely house had been hit. Her mum and dad were trying to find their beautiful furniture under the rubble and were putting what they could find into a horse and cart. Sarah was crying but when she saw me she pretended she hadn't been. I gave her a hug.

'Hello Nellie,' Mr Cohen looked up from the rubble and smiled bravely. 'Got to keep our spirits up, you know. We can't let them get to us!' He looked up at the sky as if the Germans could hear him.

'What will you do now?' I asked Sarah.

'We'll go and stay with some of our family who live on the other side of London, away from the docks,' she said. 'Pop said this place is too dangerous because the Germans want to destroy the docks, to stop us sending ships out.'

I was horrified. Sarah leave? I wouldn't see her ever again!

'Will you come back sometimes, Sarah?' I asked her.

She shook her head. 'We won't until the war is over.'

I felt tears in my eyes. 'I'm going to miss you,' I whispered.

She gave me a big hug and started to cry again. 'Me too,' she whispered back.

'Come on Sarah, time to go.' Mrs Cohen called to her. Sarah pulled away from me.

'Shall we write to each other?' I suggested.

'Good idea!' She looked a lot happier. 'Pop, can we give Nellie our address?'

'Of course, Sarah.' Mr Cohen was walking towards us with a piece of paper with an address written on it. 'I thought you might want it so I had it ready. I was going to pop it round to you before we left.' He smiled at me. 'Stay safe, Nellie. We'll see you again when we've won the war.'

After they'd gone we carried on picking over the bricks. The twins were looking for some pieces of shrapnel, which are bits of metal left over from the exploded bombs. I was just looking for anything I could find to remind me of Sarah. Maureen found a doll's head, the twins found a silver fork and began fighting over who was going to have it. Something shiny caught my eye and I began moving some of the bricks to see what it was. It was a photograph frame. All the glass had broken and the frame was a bit bent. Inside the frame was a picture of a smiling Sarah with her mum and dad. I took it out of the frame and put it in my pocket.

Desert Hero cont ...

Tex came out from under the table. Mad Man McBlaine had gone, but there were men lying everywhere, all hurt and bleeding. The room was shot to pieces. Tex called for Bella, and they began helping the injured men...

TUESDAY It was the first day back to school after the holidays. Even more people are missing from the class, although Betty White said that some of them were bunking off and playing in the rubble of the bombed houses. The Germans are still bombing night after night, and the buildings I was so used to seeing are gradually disappearing, street by street. The docks are constantly on fire, and the heat is so fierce the windows in our house are too hot to touch. The sky is black and sooty most of the time. Some people go to the air-raid shelters straight from work, with their dinner all wrapped up in cloths.

The air-raid shelters are a bit more comfortable now. Our Maureen and I usually sleep on the spice sacks that are stored there. Someone has rigged up some lights so that we can actually see each other, and there are toilets for us to use now. (It's just a pair of curtains around a bucket). As the bombs start to drop, the men from our church band play tune after tune on their musical instruments, trying to drown out the sound of the explosions. Someone usually starts singing *Roll Out the Barrel*, and gradually people join in the singing.

Our Maureen always takes Edna Daffodil with her, and Frank plays with his string and penknife most of the time. He also has some shrapnel and he does swapsies with his mates. I take my journal and my novel. I always wear my Ovaltineys badge even though I don't play with Mary O'Reilly anymore. I really miss Sarah, so being a member of the Ovaltineys makes me feel part of something, as if I'm helping the war effort, and I really enjoy cracking the secret codes at the end of the Ovaltiney show on Sunday evenings.

Desert Hero cont ...
Tex was counting his winnings in the saloon. He'd made quite a lot of money, but still not enough to buy his ranch.
Dave, the bartender, was picking up the broken chairs and sweeping the debris off the floor. He looked miserable.

"I don't know if I can afford to go on," he said. "This is all going to cost a fortune to replace."
Tex handed Dave his winnings. "A town ain't a town without a saloon bar, Dave. You'd better have this."
"Thanks Tex," said Dave, smiling. "You're a true gent."

THURSDAY Miss Robinson has said that the rest of the school are going to be evacuated to the country.

'It's not safe here for you, children,' she said. 'We're going on a train tomorrow to stay in the countryside.' She gave us all a letter to give to our mums.

It was really exciting to be going on another holiday with Mum and the others. It will be good inspiration for my novel. It's really hard trying to imagine you're in the Wild West when everything around you is made of brick and you can hardly see the sky. I might see some horses as well so I can practise drawing Silver Mist. The only horse I see at the moment belongs to Alf, the coal man. It's a great big thing with enormous legs and shaggy feet – not exactly a stallion.

When I got home I gave my letter to Mum. She read it from top to bottom without stopping. The baby began to cry but she ignored him.

'It doesn't give me much time to get your stuff ready,' she said sadly.

'I'll give you a hand with the food,' I offered. 'And you can get everyone's clothes ready.'
Mum shook her head. 'Nellie, it's not like the last time we were evacuated. This trip's been organised by the school and they're only taking schoolchildren. There isn't time to find places to stay for whole families. I won't be going with you.'

'But who will look after us?' I asked.

'Your teacher, Miss Robinson is going, so she'll make sure you're all right. You'll stay with another family and they'll take care of you.'

'But what about the twins? They're so naughty, you're the only one they'll listen to. And how will our Maureen cope without you? She'll be so miserable.'

Mum thought for a while. 'I don't think I'm going to send them,' she decided.

Frank looked surprised.

'But Mum, why can't I stay as well?' he said.

'No Frank, I need you to look after Nellie. I'll try and arrange for us to follow you down just as soon as I've found somewhere for George and Jean to stay.'

'But I want to stay here and fight the Germans!' Frank wailed. 'Please don't make me go, Mum!'

The twins came in from the yard and bashed into my stomach on purpose. 'We'll fight the Germans for you, Frankie. Pow! Pow! Splat on the floor! They won't dare come in here!'

Paul had made a gun out of a bit of old tin, and Peter was firing paper bullets from his catapult. One nearly hit me right in the eye.

'Ow, Mum, stop him, will you?' I shouted. 'He'll have my eye out!'

'Give me that thing, you little so and so,' Mum grabbed the catapult and hit him on the backside with it. 'Now go outside and fight the Germans there.'

'I think you should send the twins to Germany,' I told her. 'I reckon they're more than a match for Hitler.'

Our Maureen began to cry. 'I don't want to sleep by myself in the bed,' she blubbed. 'My feet will get cold if I can't put them on Nellie's legs.'

I gave her a cuddle. 'You'll be fine, our Maureen,' I said. 'Just keep your socks on.'

When Mum first said only Frank and I were going, I was really upset, but now I've thought about it, life without our Maureen's freezing cold feet, and not having to put up with the terrible twosome every day has started to make me feel pretty good about going away.

'Frank, you need to promise me that you'll look after Nellie,' Mum said. 'Make sure you stay together. I can't bear the thought of her being by herself in a strange place.'

'All right, Mum,' Frank agreed, but he wasn't too happy about it.

94

Desert Hero cont ...

The door opened and Bella came in. "The sheriff is rounding up a posse to capture Mad Man McBlaine, are you coming, Tex?"

Mad Man

Tex shook his head. "This isn't my fight," he said. "I'm just passing through."

"Not your fight?" Bella was astounded. "It's everyone's fight! These men have to be stopped. We can't let them keep carving up our town!"

FRIDAY

When we got back from the air-raid shelter this morning there was just time to have a wash and get our things together. George stayed at home from work to see us off. He shook Frank's hand and gave me a cuddle.

'Look after yourself, Nellie. I'll miss you. And try and stay out of trouble, Frank.' Frank grinned.

Mum left the younger ones with George and she walked Frank and me to school. More houses had been hit in the night and there were the usual fire engines out and about. We had our hats and coats on, even though it was hot, and our gas masks hanging round our necks. We also had a label pinned to our coats with

95

our name and address in case we got lost.
During the night Mum had made us both a
knapsack to put our things in.
This is what I had in my knapsack:

My journal
My Ovaltiney book and badge
My pencil box
My paint box and brushes
Socks x 3 pairs
Knickers x 3
Vests x 2
Jumpers x 2
Dress x 1
Bread and dripping x 2 slices
Marbles x 12

EVACUATION LONDON COUNTY COUNCIL

NAME *Eleanor Walker*
ADDRESS *32 Riverside Mansions*
Wapping, London

My label

Mum held my hand as we walked down the street. Frank walked the other side of her, not holding her hand, but he was very close to her.

When we got to the station, Frank ran off to meet his mate, Paddy, and I had Mum all to myself for a few minutes.

'I'll write to you Nellie,' she said, 'and I'll try and get down and see you once you've settled. Be a good girl for the people that look after you, won't you? And go to church regularly.'

I nodded as a big tear came out the corner of my eye and rolled down my nose. Mum got her hankie out and wiped it away, then blew her own nose.

'It's not forever, love, and I can rest easy knowing you'll be out of harm's way,' she said.

She walked me to the train where Frank was waiting. 'Don't forget to stay together, Frank!' she called as we were pushed on to the train.

The train was already full to bursting, and I tried to push my way through to find a seat near the window so that I could wave goodbye to Mum. But everybody else was doing the same thing and I couldn't get a look-in. By the time I squeezed my way through, the train had left the station and Mum was nowhere to be seen. I hadn't said goodbye. I felt a big lump in my throat.

'Chin up, Nellie,' Mrs Robinson said kindly. 'We've all got to do our bit for the war effort.'

'Well, going to the country isn't doing much for the war effort, is it?' said Frank gruffly. 'It's like we're just running away.'

Desert Hero continued ...
  Tex galloped away from the town, up towards the hill. He looked back and saw the townsfolk sadly waving goodbye to him.
  "Am I doing the right thing?" he asked himself...

Later on Friday - We were on the train nearly all day. I ate my bread and dripping when my stomach started rumbling, which was about five minutes after the train left. After that I looked out of the window and watched the streets full of bombed-out buildings turn gradually to green fields and tall trees. It looked so peaceful; you could easily imagine the war had never started. Then I got bored with green fields and fell asleep, and finally woke up when the train was puffing to a halt.

'Are we there yet?' I said. Miss Robinson was standing over me.

'Not yet, Nellie,' she smiled. 'We're just having a break to stretch our legs and have something to eat.'

As we got off the train, we were led into a hall near the station where some ladies had made us some tea and jam sandwiches. We were allowed to run around on the grass near the station to stretch our legs. It gave me a chance to see who was being evacuated from my class. I spotted Agnes and Marjorie sitting together. They're best friends, as well as cousins. Then I saw Mary O'Reilly standing by herself. Most of the boys were there, including Slimy Simon. We call him that because he's always got two slimy trails of snot pouring from his nose. He never uses a hankie, he just cuffs it on his sleeve. He's not a nice boy. Nobody likes sitting next to him.

After our break it was time to get back on the train.

'How much further, Miss?' Frank asked Miss Robinson.

'It's quite a few more hours yet, Frank.' She said. 'Try and keep yourselves busy with some quiet games and stay out of trouble.'

It was almost dark outside when we reached our station. The inside of the train was just as dark — the blackout meant that we couldn't have any lights on. Lots of other schools had got off before us and the train was almost empty. Some people were stretched out asleep on the seats.

Then at last a guard shouted, 'Torwenno station! Welcome to Cornwall!' followed by Miss Robinson shouting, 'All the children from St. Mary's school, Wapping, get your things together and wait quietly until I tell you to get off the train!'

'Wait for me, Frank,' I said as he went to run ahead. 'You told Mum you'd make sure we stayed together.'

'As if I could forget,' he mumbled grumpily. I think he regretted making that promise.

Once we were off the train we had to walk in a crocodile down a road to a building that had a sign on the front that said:

TORWENNO VILLAGE HALL

This was called the BILLETING HALL. Inside was a large room full of chairs in rows that we were made to sit on. I grabbed hold of Frank's sleeve so that we didn't get separated.

'Now everyone, sit nicely,' said Miss Robinson. 'Some people will come in and choose you to go and live with them. Make sure you don't cause any trouble or you'll be the last to be picked.' She looked at Frank

100

when she said that, but he didn't notice
because he was looking up at the ceiling,
whistling.

Lots of people came in and stared at us, as
if we were animals at the zoo. They said
things like, 'Oh what a pretty child, we'll
have her.' Or, 'He looks like a strong boy.'
Mary O'Reilly was the first to be picked.

No-one said anything like that to me. I
forgot to mention that, as well as my funny
knee and my difficult hair I have a STYE in
one of my eyes at the moment. In fact I have
a stye a lot of the time. In case you don't
know, a stye is like a great big yellow pus
boil that sits in the corner of your eye,
near your nose. You get them if you don't eat
enough fruit. Styes are pretty difficult to
ignore and the people in the hall seemed to
be staring straight at mine. They didn't
even try to be polite and pretend they hadn't
noticed it.

I tried smiling at people in an appealing
way. Lots of people smiled at Frank and said
what a fine-looking boy he was, and what
lovely teeth he had. But when I put my arm
through Frank's to show them that we were
together they would look away and quickly
move on.

Suddenly my stomach began to make growly
noises. I needed the toilet badly. I tried to
sit still but I couldn't stop jigging about.
I put my hand up.

'What is the matter, girl?' One of the organising ladies came over to me.

'Please miss, I need the lav.'

She sighed an enormous sigh and then took me down a corridor to a blue door.

'Here it is,' she said. 'Now, hurry up or you'll get left behind.'

I must have been in there a lot longer than I realised because, by the time I got back into the hall it was virtually empty. I looked round for Frank and saw with horror that he'd gone, and so had Miss Robinson!

'Come along girl, what's the matter?' said the grumpy organising lady who had shown me the lav.

'My brother's gone, Miss.' I gasped. 'And my mum said we were to stay together!'

'Well it can't be helped now,' she said. 'Sit down there and wait your turn.' There was only one other child left and that was Slimy Simon.

The ladies sat us together on the stage while they put all the chairs away. There we sat, the last two children that nobody wanted. Slime Boy and Pus Girl. I don't think I've ever felt so miserable in all my life.

'What are we going to do with them, Glynnis?' Grumpy organising lady said to another lady as she swept the floor. 'I've got to get home and put the dinner on.'

'I'm not sure, Eunice,' Glynnis replied, handing her the dustpan. 'We've never had any left over before.'

Then just at that moment the door flew open and a woman came in. She had a large round face with a smile so wide it took up half of her face. Her eyes were so crinkled up with smiling you could hardly see what colour they were. Later I found out they were deep blue. Her hair was a bushy golden mane that framed her head and made her look like a walking sunshine. She was simply wonderful! I held my breath, hardly daring to hope that she might pick me.

'Sorry I'm late ladies,' she panted. 'The tractor got stuck up at the top field and we had to dig it out.'

'Hello Mabel,' said Glynnis. 'I'd quite forgotten about you.'

'There's not much left I'm afraid. Just these two now,' said nasty old Eunice.
I closed my eyes tightly so that she wouldn't see my stye and I prayed to Jesus.

'Please Lord, let her pick me..'

'Open your eyes then little one, let's get a good look at you,' I heard Mabel say.
I opened the one without the stye first.

'Now the other one,' she said gently.
I tried to open my pus eye but my eyelids had stuck together.
She didn't look away, she smiled at me. I began to smile back. Then she looked at Simon's slime and smiled at him too.

'Goodness me, Eunice, if two children were ever in need of fresh air and sunshine it must be these two, and I've got plenty of that where I live.' She lifted up my chin and looked at my stye. 'Give your eye a wipe, my lovely, and come along with me. You too, young man.' Slimy Simon and I jumped up and grabbed our things quickly in case she changed her mind.

Life is very different here at Sunnyvale Farm in Cornwall. Slimy Simon and I have really landed on our feet. Aunty Mabel (the lady that collected us from the billeting hall) took us back to her farm on her horse and cart. The horse is called Ned and he is beautiful. He's white, but they don't call him a white horse, he's called a grey. He looks just like I imagine Silver Mist in my novel.

Aunty Mabel

'Can I stroke him?' I said to Aunty Mabel when I first saw him outside the village hall.

'Of course you can,' Aunty Mabel replied. 'Perhaps you'd like to have a go at riding him while you're here.' I just couldn't believe it! Me, learn to ride!!!

I quickly jumped up on the seat next to her, leaving Slimy Simon to sit at the back, and I found myself telling her all about my novel. She didn't laugh or anything, she just nodded and mmmd as if she met a budding author every day of the year.

'I think it would be good research to ride Ned,' I told her. 'Then I would know how Tex feels.'

105

On the way to the farm we peered into the darkness to see what Aunty Mabel described as fields full of corn and wheat.

'It's nearly harvest time,' she told us. 'We have to cut the crops soon. It's a very busy time. Lucky you're here to help.'

I felt a bit worried. 'I don't know how good I'll be at chopping that lot down, Aunty Mabel,' I said. 'But I'll give it a go.' Aunty Mabel laughed and her blue eyes disappeared again. She threw back her head which made her hair bob around her face like a cloud in the wind.

'We've got people to do that, Nellie,' she said. 'But they'll need feeding and it means I'm really busy in the kitchen. You can help me there. And you, Simon, can run errands for the workers. They can do with a fast runner to help them out.'
Simon looked at his skinny, white legs and bony knees and frowned. 'I don't know if I'm that fast,' he said. 'And I think I might have hay fever.'
Aunty Mabel laughed again, and so did I. Simon's nose ran all the time at home and there wasn't a single bit of hay to be seen there.

Aunty Mabel and her husband, who we call Uncle Ray, live in a large farmhouse with yellow shutters and a green front door which has pink roses growing around it.

Uncle Ray is shorter than Aunty Mabel, and he has red curly hair and green eyes. He spends most of the day in his fields, looking after the crops in his blue tractor which he calls 'Blue Bessie'. He pats Blue Bessie and talks

to her as if she's real. Apart from his conversations with Blue Bessie, Uncle Ray isn't really a chatty person; when he does speak there are long pauses in his speech as if he's giving it a good deal of thought before he says anything. It can take quite a while for him to say a whole sentence and often Aunty Mabel jumps in and finishes it for him - a bit like this:

Uncle Ray: I thought I'd …
Aunty Mabel: Eat your lunch?
Uncle Ray: No, I thought I'd …
Aunty Mabel: Have a rest?

Uncle Ray, thinking for a moment, then
nodding: Yep, have a rest.

Another really great thing about living at
Sunnyvale Farm is that Uncle Ray has a dog
called Flossie. She's a breed called a
Border Collie and she helps Uncle Ray round
up the sheep. It's amazing to watch her.
Uncle Ray just whistles at her and she runs
around the sheep and gets them
into the sheep pen. Flossie
loves Uncle Ray and she
sits next to him when he's
driving Blue Bessie.
   'Now you're not to go
fussing her,' Uncle Ray told
us. 'She's not a pet dog,
she's a working dog. You'll
turn her soft if you give her
too many cuddles.' But I
can't help it, I've always
wanted a dog, and she's so gorgeous, so I
cuddle her when Uncle Ray's not looking.

Flossie

Aunty Mable spends all day either in the
kitchen baking lots of wonderful food, or in
the garden which is full of vegetables. The
bottom of her back garden has rows of little
white houses with pointy roofs.
   'That's where my bees live,' she warned.
'So don't go down there without me. Their
sting really hurts.'

'Why have you got bees then?' Simon asked, giving his nose a wipe with his sleeve.

'To make honey,' Aunty Mabel explained. 'I'll take you down there and show you another day. They're clever little things, but in the meantime I've got some of their honey in jars and you can have a taste, as it's tea time.'

The honey was delicious - thick and runny and very sweet. I'd never tasted it before, neither had Slimy.

'Yum,' he said smiling for the first time and tried to put his finger in the jar. Aunty Mabel whipped the jar away.

'Go and wash your hands in the sink first, both of you, and then we'll get on with tea.'

She'd already made actual home-made bread, and we had it with more honey. There was also thick creamy milk to wash it down with. I have never had such a wonderful tea in all my life.

When our eyes began to grow heavy with exhaustion Aunty Mabel took us up to our beds. We followed her up wearily, dragging our bags behind us. She opened the door to one of the rooms at the top of the stairs.

'In you go, Nellie. This is yours,' she said. I couldn't believe my eyes. I had a whole room to myself. In it was a little bed with a colourful bedspread made with different colour patches of material, filled

with feathers. On top was a big soft pillow.
The sheets were ironed and clean, and as soon
as I snuggled down I was asleep.

I was woken up the next morning by a strange
sound, like someone being strangled. I got
dressed quickly and went downstairs. Aunty
Mable was already dressed and was busy by the
cooker.
   'What was that noise?' I asked her.
   'That's our rooster,' she said. 'He starts
that racket as soon as the sun comes up.
He makes sure we all get up in time.'
   'Here's your first job,' she told me
without looking over. 'Grab the basket by the
door and go and collect some eggs for your
breakfast.'
   'What, real eggs?' I said.
   'Well, they don't lay golden ones,' she
laughed. 'You'll find them in the hen house
by the back gate.'

I've decided to write a few facts to help you
in case you ever find yourself living on a
farm.

Fact No. 1

NOT EVERYTHING ON A FARM IS PERFECT

   I was a bit wary as I went towards the hen
house. I've never been near chickens before.

'They must be a bit like pigeons,' I told myself. We had loads of those in London.

As I got closer, I counted twelve brown hens picking at the ground with their beaks. They're nicer than pigeons. Their bodies are fat and round and fluffy.

'Hello,' I said politely. 'Have you got any eggs for me?' They stopped pecking and looked at me as if they were listening to what I was saying.

Feeling a bit more confident I made my way towards the hen house, and I was almost there when suddenly, the hens made a loud squawking noise and scattered in all directions. I looked round to see what had caused the rumpus and there, behind the hen house, was the biggest chicken you could ever imagine - it was almost as tall as our Maureen. It looked straight at me with unblinking eyes of pure evil. I gulped and tried to make a friendly clucking noise, but it just stood there, watching me. I kept clucking and walking towards the hen house. It still watched me, unmoving. Then, just as I was about to open the hen house door, there was a

111

loud squawking and flapping of feathers and the enormous chicken flew at me and pecked at my legs, over and over again. I screamed and threw the basket down, and ran back towards the house. My legs were bleeding and they really hurt. Someone came running towards me. It was Uncle Ray back from the fields for his breakfast.

'Are you … ?' he mumbled.

'No, I'm not all right!' I sobbed. 'That flaming chicken tried to kill me! Look what it's done to my legs!'

The back door flew open and Aunty Mable came running out looking concerned.

'What's happened?' she asked. I was still shaking with shock.

'She'll be fine,' Uncle Ray said. 'We're going to go back in the hen house together and get the … '

'I'm not going back in there, you must be joking!' I shrieked hysterically.

'You mustn't let the old rooster get the better of you,' Uncle Ray said. 'He's just protecting his ladies. You've got to show him who's boss. Just walk behind me and you'll be fine.'

Uncle Ray picked up the basket and walked towards the hen house. Then he put his arms out and started flapping them as if he were a giant chicken. Even though I was still upset, it was funny to see him looking so ridiculous. The rooster began to move

112

backwards out of the way. Then Uncle Ray put his foot firmly under the rooster's bottom and lifted it up high, as if he were gently kicking a football in slow motion.

'Gellllooooouuuuuuttttttt you … ' Uncle Ray shouted, and then miraculously the rooster ran off squawking.

'Get the eggs now,' Uncle Ray nodded towards the hen house. I quickly nipped in and found twelve, warm, brown eggs lying together in a box filled with hay. I put them in my basket and ran out as fast as I could, back up the path to the back door and into the safety of the kitchen.

'I'm really sorry Nellie,' Aunty Mabel said as I came in. 'I didn't think the rooster would be that bad. We're so used to him and his ways.' She dabbed at my peck marks with a flannel. It really hurt. Flossie was standing guard by me and gave my knee a "get-well" lick.

I had one of the eggs with home-made bread soldiers. It was lovely but I'm not sure it was worth getting pecked to death for.

Later that evening, when we were having our supper, I asked Uncle Ray what the chickens' names are.

'They haven't …'

'… got names,' continued Aunty Mabel.

'Why has the tractor got a name when it's not real, and the chickens don't and they are real?'

Aunty Mabel smiled. 'Would you like to name them, Nellie?'

Slimy started to whinge, 'Why can't I name them?'

'You can name the chickens if you like,' I said. 'But I want to name the rooster, and I've got a really good name for him.'

'What's that?' Aunty Mabel asked.

'ADOLPH HITLER!'

Desert Hero continued ...

There was a thunder of hooves, and a cloud of dust appeared at the end of the street. It was Mad Man McBlaine and his gang riding back into town. Mad Man had an evil glint in his eye and he was looking for trouble...

Fact No. 2
VEGETABLES ARE DIRTY

My favourite food from home:

Bread and dripping
Stew and dumplings
Irish stew
Fish and chips
Pie mash
Saveloy, pease pudding
and faggots

I've already told you that Aunty Mabel is an amazing cook, but there are some things she puts on my plate that I'm not too happy about. And worst of all is where she gets them from.

Aunty Mabel's garden doesn't have much grass. It has large dirt rectangles with grass paths in between them. Aunty Mabel says the dirt rectangles are called vegetable beds. In these vegetable beds are great big green plants that she pulls up.

'This is called cabbage, Nellie,' she told me. 'We cook it and eat it. It's very good for you.'

115

Now I'm not saying I know everything about everything, but I do know it's WRONG to eat food that's been on the floor, especially if it's been stuck in the mud.

'I'm not eating that,' I told her firmly. 'That's disgusting! It's covered in dirt, and there's loads of spiders and things in it!' Aunty Mabel sighed. 'It's not dirt, Nellie. We call it earth, and most food is grown in the earth. It's nature's way.'

'Well it isn't where I come from,' I said. 'We get our food from the shop or the market.'

'And the shopkeeper gets it from the farmer, who grows it in the earth,' she insisted.

It appeared on my plate that evening, but I pushed it politely to the side.

'Now eat up your cabbage Nellie,' Aunty Mabel said. 'It's been washed and boiled, and there's nothing nasty in it.'

'But it's a strange colour, Auntie Mabel,' I objected. 'Food is supposed to be brown, like bread pudding and sausages and cake. This is not natural.'

Another sigh from Aunty Mabel. 'Green is the most natural food colour in the world.'

But I don't believe a word of it.

Today was the first day at our new school. Aunty Mabel got Ned out and harnessed him to the trap.

'What fantastic fun, going to school in a horse and cart every day!' I said excitedly.

Aunty Mabel soon burst my bubble of happiness. 'I'm only taking you today because you don't know where the school is yet,' she told us. 'You'll have to walk after that. I'm too busy, and besides you could both do with the fresh air. It's less than three miles.'

'But how long will that take us?' Simon wiped his sleeve across his nose and looked horrified.

'It depends how fast you walk,' Aunty Mabel replied, not at all sympathetically.

Miss Robinson was waiting for us by the front gate. I was really pleased to see her. I could see one or two familiar faces, but the children were mostly strangers who stared at us as we walked through the gate.

'We won't be having lessons with the village children,' Miss Robinson said. 'Our school will all be together in a room round the back.' There were sixteen of us from St Mary's of Wapping, all different ages. There was no sign of Frank. Miss Robinson frowned when she realised he was missing.

'Where's he living, Miss?' I asked.

'I'm not too sure,' she said. 'I'll find out later why he's not at school.'

It felt strange to be with the children from our school, but in a different place. It was even stranger to see Mary O'Reilly sitting by herself — she was usually surrounded by people who wanted to be her friend. She didn't look as smug as usual. I didn't know whether to speak to her or not. I was deciding where to sit when Mrs Robinson said, 'Hurry up and find yourself a place, lessons are starting.' At the corner of my eye I saw Slimy Simon coming towards me so I quickly plonked myself down next to Frank's mate, Paddy.

We ate our lunch in the playground, so I sat by myself and opened my lunch. Aunty

118

Mabel had packed me an enormous Cornish
Pasty, which is a folded over pie that is
full of meat, potato and carrots. I took a
small bite and had a look inside to make sure
there wasn't any green in it. Luckily there
wasn't. I went to take another bite when I
noticed Mary looking at me. She wasn't
eating anything. I shut my mouth again and
walked over to her.

   'Haven't you got any lunch, Mary?' I asked
her.
She shook her head. 'I think the lady I'm
staying with forgot to give me some,' she
said quietly. 'I'm sure she'll remember
tomorrow.'

   'Would you like a bit of mine today?'
Mary nodded. 'Thank you Nellie,' she said in
a small voice. I broke my pasty in half and
gave one half to her. I wasn't sure whether
to stay with her or not, so I decided to just
leave her to it and sit by myself.

Simon came over to me. 'Do you want me to sit
with you, Nellie?'
   'No, I don't.'
He smiled and licked the slime from his top
lip. 'You're probably feeling a bit lonely by
yourself.'
   'No, I'm not.'
His smile disappeared. 'But -'
   'Look, thanks all the same, Simon, but I
see quite enough of you as it is.'

'There's no need to be horrible about it,' he said huffily.

I wasn't being horrible, I just didn't want him to get any ideas about him and me being friends.

WEDNESDAY I'm not in Uncle Ray's good books at the moment. He went out this afternoon and left Flossie behind at the farmhouse. Aunty Mabel was with her bees and Slimy Simon was doing some errands for Uncle Ray. That meant I had Flossie all to myself!

She was lying on the floor near the stove – she's only allowed in the kitchen. I got down on the floor next to her and gave her a great big cuddle. She really loved it and she licked my face. But it was a bit uncomfortable on the cold tiles after a while. I looked out of the window to make sure Aunty Mabel was still in the garden. She was. I went to the door in the sitting room and opened it.

'Come on Floss,' I called, patting my thigh. 'Come and sit with me, it's nice and comfy in here.' Flossie got up and poked her head worriedly through the sitting room door. 'Don't worry Flossie,' I said. 'No-one will know. It'll be fine.' But she wouldn't come in, so I dragged her in by her collar. Then I sat on the sofa and patted the cushion next to me. 'Come on girl, come and have a cuddle with Nellie.' But she wouldn't come up, so I put her front paws on the sofa and then pushed her bottom up until she was on properly. It took quite a while because she was so heavy. She didn't look very happy. She kept looking at the door as if she expected Uncle Ray to walk in.

'Oh, he'll be out for ages,' I told her. 'Don't worry about him!'
Eventually she settled down and went to sleep. I sat and stroked her head. She was lovely and silky.

Then I suddenly had a really good idea. I wondered what Flossie would look like if she

was dressed up like one of Beatrix Potter's characters. Aunty Mabel had left one of her scarves on the chair, so I doubled it up into a triangle, like I'd seen Mum do, and tied it round her head. She looked completely adorable!

She gave my hand a little lick.

'But there's something missing,' I told her, making my voice sound a bit like Jean's when she does her friends' clothes and make-up. I thought for a moment.

'I know! You need a necklace to finish the look. I wonder if Aunty Mabel's got one? I'm sure she won't mind.' I patted my leg again and called Flossie as I went up the stairs.

'Do you want to come up, Floss? It's all right, no-one's here.' But Flossie just whined and looked anxious.

I tip-toed upstairs and quickly found some pearls on Aunty Mabel's dressing table. Perfect! Flossie would look so sweet in these!

We were just having another cuddle on the sofa when my luck ran out. Uncle Ray walked in the back door at that very moment, followed by Aunty Mabel. He'd forgotten his wallet and had come back for it.

'I'm sure it's in the sitting room,' I heard Aunty Mabel say. I tried to get Flossie off the sofa and hide her behind the chair, but I wasn't quick enough.

Uncle Ray went bonkers. 'My prize collie - dressed up like a girly's doll -!' he ranted and raved like a mad man.

The very long lecture I got was about:

1. Obeying house rules.
2. Respecting other people's wishes.
3. Respecting other people's property.

Actually, I got off really lightly, but poor Flossie got shouted at and shoved outside in the cold.

'You really have to understand that Flossie is not a pet, Nellie,' Aunty Mabel explained. 'If you make her too comfortable she won't work properly and Uncle Ray will have to get rid of her.'

What! Poor Flossie, live somewhere else?

'Please don't punish Flossie, Uncle Ray,' I pleaded. 'It wasn't her fault. I forced her to do it. I promise I won't bring her into the sitting room again.'

'All right then, we'll say no more …' Uncle Ray was beginning to calm down. 'But this is an end to this soppy …'

'I really, really promise,' I said. 'But can I still stroke her sometimes?'

He didn't answer and stomped outside muttering to himself, 'Dressing up … on the sofa … huh!'

Aunty Mabel went chasing after him. 'Don't forget your wallet, dear!'

Sunnyvale Farm,
Torwenno,
Cornwall.
September 1940

Dear Mum,

I hope you are all well. I am staying with some people called Mabel and Ray Lammerton. It's very nice here and I am well looked after.

I have an egg every day which I collect from the chickens, and Aunty Mabel also keeps bees in her garden. I have my own bedroom with a pink quilt made of flower material.

There are lots of fields here and different animals. I'm going to learn to ride a horse. How is our Maureen doing without me?

Lots of love
from your daughter
Nellie
xxx

I've been a bit careful about what I put in the letter to Mum. I didn't go on too much about how nice Sunnyvale Farm is, because I didn't want Mum to think I wasn't missing her. But I didn't want to tell her I was

missing her in case it upset her. I also
didn't mention that Frank wasn't with me
either in case she was worried.

WEDNESDAY I'm not too keen on the
school here. The village
children don't play with
us. They're on one side of the playground
and we're on the other. One of them, a big
girl called Rosie, made up a song and she and
her friends chant it at us:

EVACUEES,
DON'T SAY PLEASE,
AND THEIR HAIR IS FULL OF FLEAS!

'Everyone knows that evacuees are dirty and
have no manners,' Rosie informed me in a
snarling voice.
'Well, you'd better keep away from us
then,' I said fiercely, clenching my fists.
'I was going to anyway,' she said.
'Well good, clear off then.' I told her.
I always mind my P's and Q's and I
certainly don't have fleas anymore. Aunty
Mabel washes my hair with the most revolting
soap, called carbolic soap, and then she
pulls all the eggs out. It's murder! She
tugs my hair so hard she nearly pulls my
brains out.

125

Frank didn't come to school all week. Lucky
beggar! Miss Robinson says that if he doesn't
turn up on Monday she'll find out where he's
staying and pay them a visit.

Mary O'Reilly didn't bring any lunch in all
week so I shared mine with her. I had too
much anyway. She snatched it from me without
saying 'thank you', and stuffed it in her
mouth like a savage. I don't know what her
mum would have said if she could have seen
her.

Fact Number 3
FARM ANIMALS STINK!

Aunty Mabel has given Simon and me jobs to do
every Saturday morning

My jobs are:

Cleaning out the
chickens
Mopping the kitchen
floor
Stripping the
sheets off my bed
Milking the cows

Simon's jobs are:

Cleaning out the
cows
Beating the rugs
Stripping the
sheets off his bed
Milking the cows

Uncle Ray has six cows and they're called:
Talulah, Beamish, Avis, Mavis, Lily and Rita.

I'm not mad about cows. I don't mind them
when they're in the fields, in the far
distance, but when Uncle Ray brings them in
for milking, that's just too close for

comfort.   Have you ever been close-up to a cow? THEY'RE ENORMOUS!

So you can imagine I wasn't too thrilled when Uncle Ray said we had to learn to milk them.

'You have to be careful of them kicking out,' he said as he sat me down on the milking stool beside Mavis. 'Don't get behind them, and watch that front leg.'

'Are you sure I should be doing this, Uncle Ray?' I asked anxiously. 'I'm only a little girl, remember.'

'You'll be …' he said.
Fine? Not fine? Killed?

I did get the hang of it after a while and it was beginning to be fun, when something really terrible happened.   I didn't really want to write about it in my journal, but Miss Robinson says that every experience is valuable to a writer.   Aunty Mabel says I'll look back on it one day and laugh, but I know, however old I am, even if I'm ninety, I'll never, ever find this funny.

I've decided to write it as a play so that I can pretend it happened to someone else:

The Abominable Cow Incident

Cast
Mavis – a cow
Kathryn – a pretty girl
Simon – a boy with a snotty nose
Uncle Ray – a man who is **supposed** to be in charge of the cows.

The scene is in a cowshed. Simon is hanging about, not doing very much. Uncle Ray is getting rid of dirty straw. Kathryn is expertly milking Mavis. She is sitting on a little wooden stool. There is a bucket under Mavis's udders for catching the milk.
Suddenly – Mavis fidgets and shifts away slightly from Kathryn.
Kathyrn puts her head further underneath the cow.
At that exact same moment, Mavis does a poop. The poop is dropped from quite a height, and is wet and runny. It narrowly misses Kathryn's head as it falls quickly down onto the stone floor.
As it lands, it splatters. It splatters in every direction – up, down, sideways, outwards, inwards. It mostly splatters in Kathryn's face – into her eye – on her cheek – into her hair- and also onto her arm and leg.

Kathryn holds her breath in shock and disbelief.
Then Mavis begins to wee.
A warm waterfall, gushing, splashing everywhere.
Before Kathryn has managed to get out of the way it has soaked her dress – hair – boots.
Some even goes into Kathryn's mouth as she screams.
Kathryn: Aaaaaaaarrrrrrrhhhhhhhh!!!!!!!!!!!!!!!!!!!!!!!!!!!!!!!!!!!
Kathryn jumps up and hops from foot to foot, waving her arms madly.
Uncle Ray rushes across the cowshed towards Kathryn when he sees what's happened.
Uncle Ray begins to smile, oblivious to Kathryn's shame and humiliation.
Uncle Ray: Kathryn … Kathryn!
Kathryn: *(hysterically)* I stink! I stink!
Uncle Ray begins to laugh a great big belly laugh that makes him shake like a mad jelly.

Simon comes over, laughing like a tortured hyena. Snot bubbles in his nose.
Simon: Oh my God! … this is the best day of my life! Wait till I tell everyone at school!
Kathryn: *(grabbing Simon by the throat)* If anyone else hears about this, you're a dead man!

We will never mention this incident again, other than to say there is no smell in the world worse than cow poop.

Except chicken poop.

IS IT REALLY STILL ONLY SATURDAY AFTERNOON?

Aunty Mabel looks after the chickens during the week, but on Saturday afternoons they have to have a proper clear-out, and I have been given this wonderful job. I have to go into the hen house, pick up all the chicken poop with a shovel and dump it into the wheelbarrow. It takes me about three goes before I can even bring myself to go into the hen house, it stinks so badly. I've tried holding my nose and shovelling with one hand, but the shovel is too heavy. I actually cry and snivel the whole time I'm scooping the poop.

SUNDAY After we got back from church Aunty Mabel let Simon and me go out and play. I didn't play with Simon, of course. I got away from him as quickly as I could.

I thought I'd explore the woods, which are about half a mile away from the farm, and soon I found a narrow path that led upwards through the trees. I walked for quite a while. It was very quiet apart from some birds singing, but I wasn't scared. Then the

131

trees thinned out a bit and I could see a
tall fence. I peeped through and suddenly I
saw an enormous, spectacular castle in the
distance. 'It must belong to the King!' I
thought, amazed.

Then I saw there was a gap in the fence and
sitting just inside it was a boy. He looked
a bit younger than me. He had very light
blonde hair and he was wearing a grey blazer
with a tie and some grey shorts. His cap was
on the ground by his feet. His face looked
really sad.

'Hello,' I said shyly.
He jumped about six feet into the air.

'Sorry,' I said. 'I didn't mean to frighten
you.'

'I'm not frightened,' he said quickly.
'Especially not of a girl.' He spoke
differently to me. Very posh, like the
Ovaltiney children and the King.

'Do you live here?' I asked him. 'Are you
a prince?'
That made him laugh and I could see his eyes
were green. 'No, I'm not a prince,' he said.

'Well, how come you live in such a big
house. Do you have an enormous family?'
He shook his head. 'No, I really live in
Finchley in London. I go to boarding school.
My father travels around a lot and usually my
mother goes with him, but now he's in the
Navy. My school has been evacuated to this
castle.'

I whistled an impressed whistle.

'I'm from London as well,' I told him. 'Wapping. I've been evacuated with my school but I'm staying with Aunty Mabel at Sunnyvale Farm.'

'How nice, to have an aunt in the country,' the boy said.

'She's not really an aunty. I didn't know her until recently. That's what you call adults that look after you. It's polite, see?'

He nodded. 'I understand,' he said.

'What's your name?' I asked him.

'Nicholas,' he replied. 'Nicholas Oliver Worthington.' It sounded very grand. Much grander than Nellie Walker.

Nicholas

'What's your name?' he asked me.

I hesitated for a second. Nellie didn't sound very grand, and he might then call me smelly Nellie, and I'm fed up with that. But then a thought came to me.

Nellie might not be a grand name, but my real full name actually sounded pretty posh if you said it in the right way.

'Eleanor Jane Walker,' I said proudly.

'Eleanor? I like that name. My grandmother is called Eleanor.' I felt a bit nervous that I'd called myself Eleanor, as if I'd told a lie.

'Do you often sit here?' I asked him.

'Yes, I do," he said. 'I like to imagine that I'm going through the gap in the fence and I'm exploring the woods by myself. We're not allowed out of the school premises by ourselves.'

'Do you always do as you're told?'

He looked horrified. 'Of course I do. Don't you?'

I didn't answer him. I got a couple of apples out of my pocket that Aunty Mabel had given me.

'Do you fancy one?' I asked him.

Nicholas's eyes lit up. 'Yes, please,' he said. 'Rations are a bit mean in school.'

We munched away for a bit and then Nicholas told me about himself. He wasn't very happy at school; he missed his mother, and he hadn't made any friends. I told him about my family, and about Sarah and her house being bombed.

Although Nicholas didn't live too far away from Wapping, his life was very different from mine. He only had one brother, and his family had other people to do the washing and cleaning, and make the dinner. He had lots of toys and a big garden to play in, with a tree house. It all sounded brilliant.

134

'That's why I don't want to be here,' he said gloomily.

I thought I'd see if he was an Ovaltiney, so I did the Secret High Sign.

'What are you doing?' he asked me.

'It's the Ovaltiney secret greeting. Aren't you a member?

'I've never heard of the Ovaltineys, he said. 'What are they?'

I couldn't believe he'd never heard of them. I was about to tell him when we heard voices. Nicholas jumped up.

'I'd better get back,' he said. 'I'm here as often as I can get away. Will you come and meet me again?'

'I'd like that,' I replied. Nicholas shook my hand like adults do.

'I'm very pleased to make your acquaintance, Eleanor,' he said.

'Likewise,' I answered.

'See you next week then.'

I watched him disappear through the gap in the fence, then I made my way back through the woods. I was really excited. I had a secret friend! I decided not to tell anyone about him.

SUNDAY Auntie Mabel hadn't heard of the Ovaltineys either, but I managed to persuade her to

135

let us listen to the Ovaltiney programme on the wireless this evening. Uncle Ray came in to listen as well and I think they both really enjoyed it.

'Well, blow me,' he said. 'Stories and songs for children on the … whatever next?' Of course none of them could work out what the secret message was.

'Can I look at your code book, Nellie?' Slimy Simon asked.

I shook my head. 'I'm afraid you can't if you're not a member, Simon. It's against the rules, you know.'

'What does Simon have to do to be a member, Nellie?' Aunty Mabel asked.

'You have to buy a jar of Ovaltine and I send off the paper on the inside of the lid, and then he can get one of these, I tapped at my badge importantly. 'But you would have to send off for that as well. You don't get it straight away.'

'Can you do that, Mabel?' Uncle Ray asked. 'Get some of this …'

'Ovaltine!' Simon and I finished for him.

'Does that mean I can be an Ovaltiney, Uncle Ray? Simon was all excited.

I had mixed feelings about Simon being an Ovaltiney. I didn't really want him to be the only person I could do the secret signs with, but on the other hand, I would only need two other people to become members and

then I could be a senior member and get a
silver badge!

MONDAY Frank still wasn't at school
today. I managed to speak to
Miss Robinson just before
playtime.

'I have enquired, Nellie,' she said. 'And
the billeting lady said she would give me the
address of where he's staying. I'm just
waiting to hear from her. I have to admit,
I'm a bit concerned that he's still not at
school today though.'

I've been thinking about whether I should
give Simon's disc to Mary O'Reilly when it
comes. I did promise I would help her become
a senior member, but we've fallen out since
then and I don't know if that promise still
stands.

Mary didn't bring any lunch again today.
She's beginning to look a bit strange. Her
hair is dirty and she keeps scratching. I
think she might have fleas. I'd already
asked Aunty Mabel for some extra lunch this
morning because I had a feeling Mary might
not have any again.

'Goodness Nellie,' Aunty Mabel said. 'Is
your stomach a bottomless pit?' But she put
in another sandwich anyway.
I gave it to Mary, plus some more of mine.
She ate it again as if she were starving.

137

I felt a bit sorry for her, so I decided to offer her the Ovaltiney disc. To my surprise she refused it.

'It's all right, Nellie, you keep it,' she said quietly. 'I'm not interested in the Ovaltineys anymore.'

Now I *was* worried. I thought I'd ask her a few questions to find out what was going on.

'What's it like where you're staying?'

She shrugged. 'Oh, it's all right.'

'What's the lady like that you're staying with?'

'Oh, she's fine.'

'Have you got somewhere nice to sleep?'

No answer.

I gave up in the end because she clearly didn't want to be my friend so I walked off and played by myself.

Desert Hero cont ...

Mad Man sneered at Bella. "Where's your
boyfriend gone? Too chicken to hang around?"
"He's not my boyfriend," Bella answered
bravely.

"Well, he won't mind if I do this then!" Mad
Man picked Bella up and slung her over his
shoulder. He climbed on his horse, threw her
across his saddle and galloped off.

"Sheriff! Find Tex and get him to
rescue me!" Bella shouted through the dust...

TUESDAY When I got home from school I
had a brilliant surprise.
Aunty Mabel had saddled up Ned.
'I thought you might like to have a riding
lesson,' she said. 'I've borrowed some proper
riding clothes for you. They're on your bed,
so go upstairs and put them on.'
'This is the best day of my life!' I
shouted excitedly as I went upstairs and
changed into a short-sleeved shirt and some
special riding trousers that are called
jodhpurs. The jodhpurs felt a bit strange
and baggy around my hips but the black riding
boots were a perfect fit.

Aunty Mabel helped me up onto the saddle and put my foot into the stirrup. I swung my other foot over Ned's back and held onto the reins, just like Johnny Mack Brown does in the films.

'Look at me, Simon!' I shouted as he walked into the yard. 'Do you want a go afterwards?'

'No thanks,' he grunted. 'I think I'm allergic.'

'Please yourself, you don't know what you're missing!'

'Concentrate Nellie,' said Aunty Mabel. 'Give Ned a little kick and say, "walk on"'.

I did and I couldn't believe it, Ned started moving!

Then something strange happened. My head felt all weird and spinny and the ground seemed to come up at me. I felt sick and closed my eyes.

The next thing I knew I was on the hard floor of the yard and Aunty Mabel was pushing my head between my knees. My arm really hurt as well.

'You fainted, Nellie,' she said. 'It must have been the movement of the horse that upset your balance. Then you fell off.'
Simon was laughing at me. AGAIN.

'You great booby!' he said. 'You're too scared to ride a horse!'

'No, I'm not,' I said crossly. 'You shut up, snot face!'

'Now, now you two,' said Aunty Mabel gently.

'My arm hurts,' I whimpered.

'It might be broken,' she said. 'I'd better call for the doctor. What a nuisance, Nellie. I'm so busy today. We've extra workers bringing the harvest in and I could have done with a hand making their tea.'

'I'm sure Simon could help, Aunty Mabel,' I suggested. Simon's face fell.

'Good idea! Simon, take Nellie inside and put her on the sofa. I'll put Ned away.' Simon tried to put his arm round me but I pushed him away. 'I can manage, thank you.'

'Suit yourself, booby,' he said running off.

Luckily it was my left arm so I can still write my novel and my journal.
The doctor said I have a nasty sprain and wrapped it in a bandage. Then he put a sling around my neck and tucked my arm inside.

'It'll take about a week before it feels better,' he said. 'Try not to move it around too much.'

'Why did I faint though?' I asked him.

'Being on a moving horse is a strange sensation when you've never done it before.

Your brain didn't quite know what to make of
it, I expect.' He stood up. 'Don't worry,
you'll be fine next time.'

I had to have my dinner cut up for me and
Simon laughed and called me a booby again.
   'Ignore him, Nellie. He's just being
silly,' Aunty Mabel said.
I'll silly him when both my arms are working
properly again.

THURSDAY My arm's beginning to feel a
bit better, but I'm not in a
hurry to try riding Ned again.
Aunty Mabel hasn't mentioned it since.

I met up with Nicholas. He was waiting for
me in the same place. I told him more about
the Ovaltineys and he was really impressed.
   'I wish we had Ovaltine at school, then I
could be an Ovaltiney as well,' he said. He
sounded so disappointed, I made the decision
to make him an honorary Ovaltiney. I think
it might be against the rules, but how is
Uncle Johnny and the other Ovaltiney people
going to find out?
   'I'll make you a badge out of cardboard and
write you out a little book with the secret
code in!' I told him.
Nicholas was really excited. 'We can leave
each other secret notes then!'

'We could do it every week!' I said. 'What day shall we do it?'
Nicholas thought for a bit. 'I don't always know when I'll be able to get here, but I'll come when I can.'

'I can check every day on my way home from school,' I told him.

Nicholas hasn't ever been to the penny pictures, nor has he heard of Johnny Mack Brown. I know he has lots of toys and lives in a castle, but I'm beginning to feel a bit sorry for him.

I've taught him how to play cowboys and Indians. I was Johnny Mack Brown and he was the baddie, Mad Man McBlaine.

Desert Hero continued ...

The sheriff saddled his horse. "You go and find Tex," he told Dave, "and I'll form a posse. One man can't take on a whole gang – Tex will need our help."

3 Albert Gardens,
Stepney,
London.
28th September 1940

Dear Nellie,

it was so lovely to get your letter. Our Maureen loved the pictures. We are all safe and well but we've had to move house further away from the docks as our house was bombed. Nobody was hurt – we were all down the shelter.

Your dad came home. I'm sorry you didn't get to see him. He borrowed Alf's horse and cart to move what was left of our things to the new house. It's very nice. We've got much more room.

Jean is still working for the WVS and is often out all night, but she's still managing to go to work in the shop during the day.

Here's some news! George has joined the RAF! He looks very smart in his uniform. He went off to a training camp but he didn't say where it is. They're not allowed, you know, in case the Germans find out.

Our Maureen misses you, and the twins are as naughty as ever. Last week they tied your dad's shoelaces together while he was asleep in the chair, and he fell over when he stood up. He was really furious and sent them to bed without any dinner.

Is Frank alright? I haven't heard from him. I know he's not a great letter writer, but perhaps you could let me know how he's getting on.

From your loving Mum

xxx

 **SATURDAY** When I was cleaning out the stinky chickens this morning, Uncle Ray came into the garden shaking his head.

'I'm three sheep down today,' he said to Aunty Mabel.

'Foxes?' she asked.

'Must be,' he replied. 'Joe Penrose lost two a couple of days ago. Damn greedy fox. We'll have to get the shotguns and do a night watch.'

'Can I come, Uncle Ray?'

'Erm …' said Uncle Ray.

'Definitely not,' said Aunty Mabel. 'It's no place for a child, particularly a girl.'

Aunty Mabel gave me a pasty for lunch and I went to the gap in the fence to meet Nicholas. I took the cardboard badge I'd made for him as well as the little book. He was thrilled with them. I showed him how to use the secret code and we practised sending each other messages.

This is the message I wrote to him:

2 32 32 24 10   32 18 10   18 28

50 30 42 36   10 50 10,

12 24 18 6 22   18 40   30 42 40   2 28 8

46 2 40 6 16   18 40   12 24 50

(Message No 2)

Nicholas managed to work it out quite
quickly. I was really impressed. Even
though he's younger than me, he's really
clever.

   'I'm glad you're my friend, Eleanor,' he
said, eating one of Aunty Mabel's biscuits I
had brought with me. 'I don't know many
girls, and the ones I do know seem to cry a
lot and only want to play girly games. There
aren't any girls at my school; it's boys
only.'

   'I've got both at my school, but actually I
wish it was girls only. The boys I know are
mostly horrible to me, apart from one of
Frank's friends, and he's still in London.'

   When we'd finished playing secret messages,
Nicholas told me he'd thought of a plan so
that he could go home.

   'I'm going to try and get expelled,' he
said.

   'What does that mean?' I asked.

'It means that the school don't want you anymore and they send you home.'

'But how can you do that?'

'You have to do something really naughty,' he said.

I was shocked. 'What are you going to do?'

He shook his head. 'I haven't thought of anything bad enough yet.'

Before I left we found a big rock that makes a great hiding place for our secret messages.

MONDAY Mary O'Reilly wasn't in school today. One of the village girls, Celia Dawson, said that Mary's mum had arrived and taken her home because the lady she was staying with hadn't looked after her very well and had half-starved her. It was horrible to hear that Mary had been treated badly. Now I knew why she had always been so hungry at school.

It made me worry more about Frank. Perhaps he was being treated badly too?

After lunch Miss Robinson came into the classroom looking very unhappy.

'I'm afraid I'm going to have to go back to London, children,' she said. 'My mother has been hurt in the bombing and is in hospital. I need to be with her. I'm really sorry to leave you like this, but Mr Martin, the headmaster, is going to teach you himself.'

My heart sank. I don't like Mr Martin. He's a very tall, thin man who peers at you over his glasses when he's talking. He has a long, bony nose, and his nostrils are long slits with hairs sticking out of them. His mouth is usually tight shut in a straight line. His face always looks cross, even when nobody's been naughty.

Mr Martin

Before she left, Miss Robinson took me to one side and spoke to me in a quiet voice.

'Nellie, I just wanted you to know that I tried to see Frank yesterday, but there was no answer when I knocked on the door, although I'm certain there was somebody in. It's made me a little worried about him, especially in the light of what's happened to Mary O'Reilly.' She took a small piece of paper out of her pocket. 'I've told Mr Martin about my concerns and also the billeting officers, but just in case …' she coughed slightly and looked behind her to make sure nobody was listening, ' … just in case this matter is overlooked, I would like you to write to your mother and tell her, and give her the address of where Frank is staying.

148

I've written to her myself as well, but I don't trust the post these days.' She handed the paper to me. It said:

Hallows Thatch
Hornbeam Rd.
Torwenno.
Cornwall

'The woman who lives there is called Miss Sally Nightshade. She doesn't have any other family, and Frank is the only evacuee staying with her.'

I felt fidgety all afternoon once Miss Robinson had gone and I couldn't concentrate.

Mr Martin made me write: "I must concentrate on my lessons," one hundred times as a punishment, so I was late leaving school.

On my way home from school I thought again about the strange conversation I'd had with Miss Robinson about Frank. I would write to Mum this evening, but what if she didn't take me seriously? And even if she did, what if she wasn't able to do anything about it? She couldn't just come down here with all those children. She wouldn't be able to afford the train fare anyway.

149

Then I had an amazing, fantastic idea. I would organise a RESCUE MISSION!

During dinner I asked Aunty Mabel where Hornbeam Road was.

'It's quite a walk from here, Nellie. You go up the hill as if you're going to the village, but you turn left down a track, just after the apple orchard,' she replied. 'Why do you want to know?'

I hesitated. I thought about telling her, but then I decided I couldn't trust her. I haven't really known her that long. She might know the woman who lives there and be angry if I say I think Frank is being badly treated.

'Oh, one of the village children lives there somewhere,' I lied. 'She's asked me if I want to go and play there this week.'

Aunty Mabel smiled. 'I'm glad you're finally making friends. There are some lovely girls around here.'

I felt guilty about lying to someone as nice as Aunty Mabel, but I couldn't risk telling her the truth. This was too important.

Sunnyvale Farm
Torwenno,
September 1940

Dear Mum,

I'm sorry but I told you a lie about Frank.
He isn't staying here with me at Sunnyvale Farm. We
got separated when we first arrived in the village
and I haven't seen him since.

Miss Robinson has been trying to find him but she's
had to go back to London. She went to his
address but nobody answered the door when she
knocked. I'm worried something nasty has happened to
him so I'm sending you his address in the envelope.

From Nellie
xxx

I also wrote a secret message for Nicholas:

26 10 10 40   26 10   16 10 36 10   30 28

40 42 10 38 8 2 50   2 12 40 10 36

38 6 16 30 30 24   18 40   18 38   2

26 2 40 40 10 36   30 12   24 18 12 10

2 28 8   8 10 2 40 16

(Message No 3)

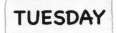

Nicholas was waiting for me by the gap in the fence. He jumped up when he saw me.

'What's going on Eleanor?'
I quickly told him what had happened. 'I need to try and rescue Frank from this Hallows Thatch place. He might be starving to death like Mary O'Reilly!'

'How do you plan to do it? You don't know if you'll be able to get in there.'

'I don't know yet, I don't know what we're up against. We'll find that out when we get there.'

Nicholas hesitated. 'We might get into trouble. I've told you I'm not supposed to leave the school grounds without permission.'

'I thought you wanted to get into trouble anyway. They're sure to send you home if you go out without permission.'

Nicholas's face lit up suddenly and he grinned a huge grin.

'Oh yes!' he said. 'I hadn't thought of that. What are we waiting for? Let's go!'

Although it was still a sunny afternoon, Hallows Thatch sat in an eerie darkness caused by the thick dense trees that grew around it.

'It looks like the cottage in Hansel and Gretel,' Nicholas whispered, as we hid behind a nearby prickly bush. 'Do you think a witch lives there?'
Although I tried not to show it, I was feeling quite scared. The cottage was very pretty, the outside was painted pink with little wooden shutters, although it looked as if it needed a new lick of paint. It looked exactly like the sort of place a witch might live.

'What if she's eaten him?' Nicholas whispered again, his eyes growing large and round with fear.

'There's no such thing as witches,' I whispered back. 'You stay here a minute, I'll have a look around and see if I can spot Frank.'

'All right then,' Nicholas agreed rather quickly. 'I'll be the look-out.'

With my heart pounding like a big bass drum, I made my way slowly around the outside of the garden. It had a high hedge but you could see through the gaps.

There, standing by a large pile of wood was Frank. He had a small axe in his hand and he was chopping firewood.

'Pssst, Frank.' I whispered as loudly as I could. 'Pssst, over here!'
Frank turned his head. 'Frank, pssst, it's me, Nellie!'
Frank looked all around him as if he was scared of something, and then he cautiously made his way to where I was psssting. He looked different, filthy dirty and really thin. His face was pure white under all the dirt, and his eyes were ringed with dark purple.

'What are you doing here Nellie?' he whispered. He kept looking behind him.

'I was worried about you, Frank. Why haven't you come to school?'

'The lady I live with, she won't let me. She makes me work all day and she locks me in the cellar if I don't do as I'm told. You have to go away Nellie, I'll get into trouble.' He looked really frightened. I was shocked. I'd never seen Frank frightened before.

'I've come to rescue you,' I told him. Is there anywhere you can get out?'

'No, everywhere's locked up. I tried, but she found out and she hit me really hard.' He

pointed to his eyes, and I realised the
purple around them were two enormous bruises.
   'Can't you pretend to threaten her with the
axe and climb out of the window?'
   'Don't be stupid Nellie,' he whispered.
'This isn't a Johnny Mack Brown film.
Suddenly a loud voice shrieked:
   'What are you doing out there? Are you
talking to someone? You'd better not be, or
it'll be the worse for you - and them!'
   A hideous looking woman with long black
hair was   standing at the door. She was
                    enormous. She was as tall
                    as a man and completely
                    filled the doorway. She
                    looked like a witch.
                       'It's nobody, Miss
                    Nightshade,' Frank
                    called back. 'I thought
                    I heard a fox, but
                    there's nothing here.'
                    He turned to me.
                    'Nellie,' he
                    whispered.
Horrible witchy woman   'There's something
                    going on here.
Something's not right …'
   'I'll be back with some help, don't you
worry.' I watched as Frank ran back to the
wood pile and started chopping wood again,
but the woman grabbed him and punched him
really hard on the ear. Then she dragged him

155

inside the cottage. I could hardly breathe, I felt sick. How could this have happened to my brother? What would my mum say if she knew?

I ran back to Nicholas. 'I've seen Frank but I couldn't get him out,' I panted. 'Frank is in a state even worse than Mary O'Reilly. He's in actual *danger!* Nicholas, Frank is being held captive by a witch!

By the time I got back to Sunnyvale Farm the house was empty apart from Simon. He was on the sofa in the sitting room, eating cake. He was getting crumbs everywhere.

'Where's Aunty Mabel?' I said.

'Gone out to see her friend. She won't be back till late. Uncle Ray's gone out to try and catch foxes. Said something about losing more sheep.'

'You're not supposed to eat in the sitting room. Look at the mess you've made. Aunty Mabel will be furious.'

'I'll tell her you did it. Anyway, you're already in trouble for not getting back for supper in time.'

Some of his nose slime went onto his cake as he stuffed it into his mouth. I gagged. He's so revolting.

'Where have you been anyway?' he asked.

'Mind your own business, I said.

I didn't see Aunty Mabel until the morning. I'd decided I was going to tell her about Frank and what I'd been up to, but she was really cross with me and wouldn't let me speak.

'I don't want to hear your excuses, Nellie. Get ready and go to school. I'm really disappointed that you didn't get back for supper in time. You make sure you come home today straight from school and I'll have a load of jobs for you to do.'

'But I –'

'No more arguing, now get to school.'

Simon smirked. He really enjoyed seeing me in trouble.

I couldn't concentrate again in class and I got into a bucketful of trouble. I had to stay in at lunchtime and do more lines. This time I had to write: "I must not draw witches on my arithmetic book".

The afternoon dragged on and I couldn't stop thinking of Frank locked in a cellar, starving and hurt.

I don't know what happened to Nicholas. I didn't have time to go to the gap in the

157

fence to find out. For all I know he's
already been expelled and is on his way back
home.

After school: When I got home Aunty Mabel was in
the kitchen as usual. Uncle Ray was also
there, which was quite unusual as he is
normally in the fields. Aunty Mabel's face
was serious. She nodded towards the sitting
room.
   'You've got a visitor,' she said.
 I felt myself go all hot. My face must have
been bright red. What if it was the witch
woman, Sally Nightshade? Could she have,
through black magic, somehow managed to find
me? Perhaps she'd tortured Frank to tell him
where I lived! Or perhaps she *was* a friend of
Aunty Mabel and she'd found me that way! I
took a huge breath and walked into the
sitting room.
   But it wasn't Miss Nightshade sitting on
the sofa. It was a man, a man looking very
smart in a soldier's uniform. The man stood
up and put his arms out towards me.
   'Hello, my little Nellie Dean,' he said.
Sudden tears welled up in my eyes.
   'Dad! What are you doing here?' I threw
myself at him and nearly knocked him over.
He finally managed to unwrap my arms which
were squeezing him hard around his neck, and
stood me upright in front of him.

'Let me get a good look at my girl,' he said. 'What's going on? You're all tall and growing up! And you're as brown as a berry!'

'She eats me out of house and home,' Aunty Mabel smiled as she walked in. 'But she's no trouble ... most of the time.'
Then I remembered Frank.

'Dad, Frank's in trouble. He's a prisoner in a witch's cottage!'

'Don't panic, I've already been to the house and I've brought him here. He's fine now, he's upstairs sleeping like a baby.'
I couldn't believe it! Frank was here — safe and sound in Sunnyvale Farm!

'Can I see him?'

'All in good time,' Aunty Mabel said. 'In the meantime, why don't I pack you both a picnic tea and you can take your dad out and show him around, Nellie?'

'Thanks, Aunty Mabel, but I have to know what happened to Frank first. Dad, please tell me, what happened when you got to the cottage?'

'All right, Nellie,' said Dad sitting down again. 'Well, I was just about to go back to the army when your letter arrived, so I got straight on to my regiment and managed to get permission to have one more day's leave, and then jumped onto the next train to Torwenno, and straight to the house you wrote to us about.'

159

'What about the witch woman, did you see her?'

'The woman wouldn't answer the door, he said grimly. 'But I knew she was there. I had to break it down in the end. It took me a while to find Frank. He was in the cellar lying on a piece of dirty sack. Can you believe it? My poor lad. It was pitch dark in there. You can imagine how surprised he was to see me. He was in a right sorry state.'

'What about the witch,' I asked again impatiently. 'Did you see her?'

'Did I see her? She took a swing at me with a plank of wood! Nice way for a lady to carry on, I must say! Then she ran off, but I didn't chase after her, I was more concerned about Frank. I picked him up and carried him back to the village to find a doctor. The doctor says he's all right, nothing that a bit of rest and good food won't put right. Then a man from the village offered to bring us here in his truck.'

My eyes were gleaming with excitement. My very own dad had broken down a door and rescued Frank. He was a HERO, just like Johnny Mack Brown!

Aunty Mabel came into the sitting room with the picnic, so I took dad outside and showed him around the farm, and then into the woods. I told him absolutely everything, including about Ned and how I fell off him. I even told him about *The Abominable Cow Incident*

160

because I was enjoying seeing him laugh so much.

Dad wiped the tears from his eyes. 'You're having a fine old time,' he said. 'I'm glad you're with such lovely people. And your leg is much straighter!' I looked down and saw that he was right. The knobble is definitely smaller. I hadn't even noticed!

'It must be all the food I'm eating. I'm stuffed like a cushion every day,' I said.

'Your mum will be really pleased to hear you're getting on so well,' Dad smiled.

Dad had to go back to London that evening because he only had the one day off. Aunty Mabel and Uncle Ray had agreed that Frank could stay with us. Uncle Ray took us both into the village on the horse and cart and Dad telephoned Mum from the red phone box on the edge of the village green. Dad had arranged for Mum to be by the telephone in the post office in London at half-past four. She was overjoyed to hear that Frank would be all right; she'd been worried sick. Then it was my turn to speak to her. It was lovely to hear her voice again but I couldn't make out what she was saying because she was crying so much. Then we took Dad to the train station. When the train pulled away I waved and waved until I couldn't see him anymore.

Desert Hero cont ...

Tex had just settled down by his campfire for the night when Dave the barman appeared.

"I'm glad I found you," Dave gasped. "Mad Man Mc Blaine has taken Bella captive!"
Tex ran towards Silver Mist.

I'm coming with you, Dave!"

On the way out of the train station, PC Trescott, our village policeman, cycled towards us on his bicycle. 'Hoi, Ray, hold up! I've got some news for you! I've been over to the Nightshade place and you'll never guess what I found!'

PC Trescott told us that he'd searched the sheds in the witch's garden and  discovered loads of dead sheep hanging up, and some more packed in boxes. It turned out that they were the very same sheep that had gone missing from Uncle Ray's and other farmers' flocks. They hadn't been eaten by a fox — they'd been stolen!

'It's just like the cattle rustlers in the Johnny Mack Brown films,' I told Uncle Ray. 'They're baddies that steal other people's cows.'

'Sheep aren't cattle,' Uncle Ray replied.
'Cows are cattle.'

'So, Sally Nightshade's a sheep rustler
then?' I asked.

'Well, yes, I suppose so.'

'What was she going to do with all that
meat?' I asked.

'I expect she was going to sell it on the
black market,' said PC Trescott.

'What's the black market?' I asked.

'It's when people sell stolen goods to
other people without proper ration coupons,'
said PC Trescott.

'You mean that some people would get more
than their fair share?'

'That's exactly it, Nellie,' said Uncle
Ray. 'Now, no more questions. You've
exhausted my poor brain!'

FRIDAY I can't believe it, Frank is
still asleep! He's in my old
room and I've been put into a
room in the attic. I don't mind. I'm on a
mattress on the floor now, but it's really
comfortable, and I've still got my lovely
pink quilt. I've got a little window that I
can look out of and I can see all across the
fields to the village.

All the hay has been gathered now and it's
been rolled up into big stacks ready to be

taken to the sheds for the winter. Uncle Ray is going to begin ploughing soon and he'll plant some winter crops. Before that though, the apples need picking and storing. There's always lots to be done on a farm.

In all the excitement, I'd forgotten about Nicholas, so I went to the gap in the fence to see if he had left me a message. He had:

18   2 26   38 40 18 24 24   16 10 36 10

(Message No 4)

I waited a while to see if he would turn up but he didn't.

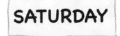 Frank finally woke up today. I found Aunty Mabel taking some breakfast up to him on a tray.
  'Can I do that?' I asked her. 'I haven't seen him properly for ages. I'm sure he'll want to see me.'
  'All right then,' she agreed. 'But don't go bothering him with lots of questions. He's had a very traumatic time and might not want to talk about it.'

164

'I won't,' I promised.

Frank was sitting up in bed when I opened the door. His face was very white and even his freckles had gone pale. You could still see the purple bruises around his eyes.

'Breakfast is served, sir.' I said grandly.

'Hello Smelly,' he grinned. 'Is that for  me? What have you got?'

I put the tray on the bed. There was a big rasher of crispy bacon, two eggs, mushrooms and a great big slice of bread, completely smothered with butter.

'I helped make the bread,' I told him. 'And the butter. You put cream into a churn and swish it about for ages until it goes thick.'

Frank's eyes nearly popped out of his head. He shovelled the food in so quickly, it was gone in a couple of minutes. I couldn't believe anyone could eat so quickly, he was even faster than Mary O'Reilly. He washed it down with a cup of tea and wiped his mouth with his sleeve.

'Did you have a really awful time, Frank?' Ooops! I didn't mean to ask him, it just came out of my mouth.

165

'Yeah, it was really horrible. She made me do all the cleaning and cooking and she hardly gave me anything to eat at all.' He shuddered. 'Then one day I was snooping around her desk and I found a list of people's names she was selling black market meat to. Worse luck, she came in at that moment and caught me. That's when she locked me up in the cellar. She only let me out if she wanted jobs done, and then she watched me like a hawk in case I tried to escape.'

'Did you see her doing any witchcraft?' I asked.

Frank looked at me as if I was mad.

'Of course not, Nellie. She's not really a witch but she's a nasty piece of work.' He shuddered for a moment, remembering. 'Then Dad turned up. I couldn't believe it! I thought I was dreaming. Where is he, by the way?'

'He wanted to stay but he said his leave was up and he would have got into trouble if he'd stayed any longer.'

Frank looked sad. 'I wanted to go back to London with him, but he said the bombing is worse than ever.'

'But the twins and our Maureen are still there!'

'I know, but who'd have the twins? They're a nightmare.'

'Mum ought to send them down to that old witch,' I said smiling. 'It'd serve her

166

right. They'd probably lock *her* in the cellar!'

Frank laughed. 'You're right, Nellie.' And then out of the blue he gave me a big hug. 'Thanks for coming to my rescue.'

I nearly fell backwards off the bed with shock. Frank had never cuddled me before.

SUNDAY   This is what Frank ate today:

Breakfast
2 eggs, 2 rashers of bacon, 2 pieces of bread and butter, 1 cup of tea.

Snack
2 biscuits and a glass of milk

Lunch
2 pieces of bread and butter, half a plate of ham, 3 tomatoes, a big wedge of cheese, a big piece of apple pie with loads of custard, large glass of milk.

Snack
apple

Supper
more bread and butter, roast lamb, roast potatoes, carrots, gravy, Spotted Dick with custard, large glass of milk.

How can one person eat this much?

PC Trescott came to speak to Frank in the afternoon. He was trying to get as much information as he could about Sally Nightshade.

'Have you arrested her?' I asked.

'Not yet, Miss,' PC Trescott said. 'She's disappeared. Probably gone into hiding with her gang,'

'Gang?'

'We don't think she was working alone. It's too big an operation for one person to manage. And ol' Sal Nightshade's not quite right in the head, so I doubt she could have thought the whole thing up by herself.'

MONDAY When I got home from school, Frank was up from bed, but Aunty Mabel made him lay on the sofa with a blanket over him.

'He was a bit bored this afternoon,' Aunty Mabel said when I came into the kitchen. 'I think he could do with some company.'

I offered to read him my novel as long as he didn't laugh at it.

'I won't,' he promised. So I sat on the edge of the sofa and read it. He was quiet all the time I was reading. I got to the bit when Tex went to rescue Bella, and I looked up. Frank was fast asleep.

'I didn't think it was that boring,' I thought, a bit miffed.

168

While Frank was asleep I thought I would write a bit more.

Tex and Dave met up with the posse and they planned to storm Mad Man's hideout, but while they were sleeping in the night, I decided to make Tex steal the Sheriff's gun and go there by himself.

Desert Hero cont ...

"This is my problem and I'll fix it," Tex thought."If I had stayed to fight, Bella wouldn't be captured now."

He jumped on Silver Mist and galloped off into the night ...

Although I haven't mentioned it to Mum in my letters, we also have air-raids in Torwenno. Even though we're a long way from any cities, there's an RAF base not too far away from us. That means that we often see our own planes flying over.   It's always scary, because you never know at first if the planes are British or German.

Sometimes there actually are German planes going over, and they drop bombs. Not always because they're trying to hit a target here, but because they have to get rid of their bombs before flying back to their airbase again. Some houses near us have been hit, and some people have been killed, but not Sally Nightshade, worse luck.

Because we live so far from the village we don't hear the air-raid siren going off, so we don't actually know about any planes coming over until we hear them,  or see them in the distance. You haven't always got time to get to the shelter so we have to take our chances and hide under the trees. We haven't had any bombs fall near the farm yet, so we've been pretty lucky so far.

Uncle Ray has dug a big hole in the garden and has built a little hut inside it. It's called an ANDERSON SHELTER.

It has camp beds in, and Aunty Mabel has put a store of food and tea in there for us. We haven't had to sleep in there yet, and I'm glad because it smells a bit damp and stinky.

I had a letter from Sarah:

19 Sweetwell Terraces
North London

Dear Nellie,

We are living with my Uncle Saul and his family. I'm
sharing a bedroom with my cousins, Leah and Rachel.
It seems that the bombing is just as bad here.

The streets change every day when we come out of
the shelters. More and more houses are blown up and
the air is black with smoke. The boys spend all day
playing in the rubble looking for shrapnel and other
treasures.

A lot of schools are closed now, but there's a house
nearby where a teacher lives and a few of us go there
every day for lessons. My mum is worried that we
may be bombed again so I think we might be moving
to the country soon.

Mum works in a factory that makes parts for
aeroplanes. It seems funny not having her there
when I get home. Dad helps out in my uncle's shop
during the day and is in the Home Guard in the
evenings. He has a brown uniform and a metal hat
and he's very proud of it.

Please write soon
Sarah xxx

It's turned a bit colder and it's getting dark earlier now. Aunty Mabel says that we are having a festival soon called ALLANTIDE. It's to celebrate the end of the summer and the coming of the winter. We've been picking and storing enormous red apples called Allan apples that we have to polish until they are shining and then we will take them to the Allan market, which is set up just to sell the apples at this time of year.

Everybody is given an Allan apple, and you are supposed to try and peel it in one go, throw the peel over your shoulder, and it will land in the shape of the first letter of your future husband's name. Obviously I won't be doing that as I have no intention of marrying anyone.

We're having a big party which is normally held outdoors with an enormous bonfire, but this year it's taking place in the village hall without the fire, because of the blackout. I'm really excited as I've only ever been to one party before, and that was Mary O'Reilly's birthday party. It's going to be a full moon as well, which makes it extra special.

We're practising some new songs at school because we're going around the village and

172

knocking on people's doors and they give you
pocket money. Everybody makes turnip
lanterns and carves out funny faces on them,
then they put a candle inside it to light up
the face. That's what they do around here.

Before the party I'm going around
the village with Rosie, the big
girl from school who said we had
fleas. She started talking to
me after the people in the village heard
about what happened to Frank. It was her dad
who gave Dad and Frank a lift to Sunnyvale
Farm from the village. Rosie told me that
Miss Nightshade was well-known for being a
bit mad, and most people don't have anything
to do with her. Also, the billeting officers
(that's nasty Eunice and her friend Glynnis)
have been told off for letting her take Frank
in the first place.

Desert Hero cont ...

Mad Man's hideout was surrounded by a high
fence. Tex found a small gap and peeped in.
There was a baddie taking some food and
water into a big shed.
  "I bet that's where Bella is," he thought ...

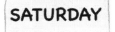**FRIDAY** Aunty Mabel has made an enormous apple cake which she says is for the party tomorrow.

Nicholas is really disappointed that his school aren't joining in the celebrations, and he's desperate to go, so we've hatched a great plan: he's going to come disguised as a boy from the village.

As soon as it gets dark tomorrow, I'm meeting him at the gap in the fence. I'm borrowing some of Simon's clothes for Nicholas to change into, then we'll go down to the village hall together. Once he's been there for a while and we've had a good time, I'll take him back to the gap in the fence and then he'll sneak back to his dormitory (that's what he calls his bedroom).

'What if you get caught?' I said.

'I don't care if I get caught on the way back, as long as they don't find me before the party!'

'That's really brave of you,' I said.

'What's the worse they can do to me?' he replied. 'Send me home? That's exactly what I want anyway.'

SATURDAY Late afternoon: when it's almost dark

I went to get some of Simon's clothes from his room but Frank caught me sneaking in.

174

'What are you doing in there, Nellie?'

'Er - nothing,' I mumbled.

'Well, clear off then,' he said. 'Simon's things are private.'

Blast!

I hung around for a while hoping that Frank would go out, but he went to his room and settled down on his bed with a comic. The door was open and he could see into Simon's room from where he was laying. I popped my head around the door.

'Are you not going to the party, Frank?' I asked all innocently.

'Not yet,' he said. Then he looked at me suspiciously. 'What are you up to?'

'Nothing,' I said and quickly went up to the attic.

Double blast!

Five minutes later: in my attic room - What can I do? I'm not going to be able to get any of Simon's clothes for Nicholas, but if I don't take something for Nicholas to wear he won't be able to come to the party because he's only got his school uniform and everyone will know that he's from the castle.

Five more minutes later:

I've had a bit of a think and there's only one thing for it.

At the gap in the fence:

'Girls' clothes?' Nicholas held up my yellow skirt in disgust.

'It was all I could get,' I replied. 'I tried to get some of Simon's clothes but Frank was hanging around and he was getting suspicious of me.'

'But people will laugh at me!'

'They won't because they'll think you're a girl.'

'Me? – pretend to be a girl?'

'What's wrong with being a girl?'

'Nothing – if you happen to be a girl.'

Nicholas was sulking and I was beginning to get impatient.

'Look, the main thing is that you go to the party, right?'

'Right,' Nicholas mumbled.

'Well, the only way you can go to the party is by dressing-up as someone else, right?'

'Right.'

'The only clothes we have for you to dress-up in are mine, right?'

'Yes, but –'

'Then take it or leave it,' I said firmly. 'If you won't dress-up, you can't go to the party.'

Nicholas thought for a moment. 'All right then,' he said grumpily. 'But don't you tell anybody.'

'Who would I tell? Nobody knows about you, you're my secret friend.'

'You'd better call me Susan then,' he decided. 'I quite like that name.'

By the time we arrived at the village hall the full moon was shining so brightly, it was a wonder they weren't trying to fly up there and drape a black-out blind over it.

Inside, everybody was laughing and dancing, and Uncle Ray was playing his harmonica on the stage, along with a band called The Torwenno Merry Players. There was a man playing the fiddle; one had a penny whistle; another played the accordion and Uncle Ray's friend, Jim Long, played a type of drum you have on your lap, which you beat with a beater that looks like a wooden spoon. The music really was merry and it made you want to join in.

Nicholas didn't want to dance though. At first we were a bit nervous about being found out, but nobody seemed to notice that he was a strange boy dressed as a girl. After a while we relaxed and began to enjoy ourselves. We ran around the hall, ducking in and out of the dancers, and then we played hide-and-seek under the tables.

There was loads to eat. Nicholas had three bits of Aunty Mabel's apple cake and two pasties, *and* he'd only just had his supper! 'You'll be sick,' I told him, sounding like a parent.

'I don't care,' he said, his mouth stuffed full of cake. It sounded more like, 'ahh, ont, eeer.'

We played BOBBING APPLES, where you put your face in a big barrel of water full of apples, and you have to try and eat one without using your hands. It was great fun and we got completely soaked.

Frank came for a while and walked round with Paddy and Simon. He doesn't seem to mind Simon, and Simon isn't as obnoxious when Frank's around. I stayed out of his way because I didn't want him noticing Nicholas.

Then suddenly we saw some serious looking people talking to the villagers, as if they were asking questions. Nicolas knew who they were though. 'Oh blast, it's Mr Lock and Miss Holsten, my teachers from school. They must have discovered I'm missing!'

'We'd better scarper then,' I said.

We charged back to the gap in the fence,
looking behind us all the way, hearts
thumping, expecting the teachers to jump out
and grab us. When we got there Nicholas
struggled in the dark to get into his own
clothes. He put his leg through the sleeve of
his blazer by mistake and fell over.
    'Ouch," he said. I've got a branch in my
armpit!'
    'Hurry up, you idiot!' I giggled. 'They'll
find us!'
    'I'll leave you a secret message and let
you know what's happened as soon as I can,'
he said and gave me one last grin before he
disappeared.

MONDAY   I went up to the gap in the
                fence and looked under our
                stone to see if there was any
message from Nicholas. There wasn't. I left
him a message asking if he'd been caught

November 1940   Still no message from
Saturday   Nicholas, and my letter was
                      still there. He must be in
                      deep trouble. I feel
really sad that he might have gone home.
Will he write to me now he's back home?

179

Two Saturdays Later

It's raining and cold and miserable today. I can see Frank from my bedroom window. He's been helping Uncle Ray in the field this week. Uncle Ray has shown him how to drive the tractor. Frank's walking towards the gate and he's got something in his hand. Now he's bending down and it looks like he's digging a hole near the fence with a trowel. What's he up to? I'm going to find out.

He'd just put the trowel down when I got there.

"What are you doing Frank?"

Frank looked a bit startled to see me, but then he put his hand in his pocket and took out some coins. I gasped.

'Where did you get those from?" I said. 'Did you pinch them?'

Frank laughed. 'No, I didn't. Uncle Ray gave me some wages for helping him plough the field.'

'That's not fair! You get to have fun driving the tractor and then you get paid for it as well!'

'I know. Great, isn't it?'

'Why are you burying it?' I asked him.

'I don't want to leave it lying about in case the Germans invade. They might steal it.'

I nodded. It seemed like a good plan.

  'It's a bit like buried pirate treasure.' I said. 'Will you make a treasure map?'

  'I hadn't planned to.'

  'Shall I draw you one?'

  'Sure, if you like, Nell.'

How to Make a Realistic Treasure Map

Soak the paper in some tea to make it look old.

Leave to dry.

Crease the paper and tear the edges a bit.

Draw the map.

When it is finished, wrap it up into a scroll and tie with a piece of string.

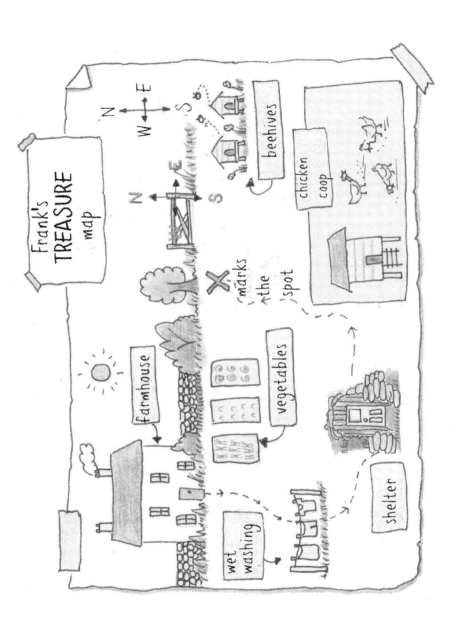

SUNDAY Life isn't so exciting now that Nicholas has gone, and there isn't anyone else to rescue. I still haven't made any more friends, not that I was particularly trying to. I'm on speaking terms with Rosie, but we don't have much in common. I don't really know what to do with myself.

Aunty Mabel found me kicking my heels in the garden.

'If you're bored, why don't you play with Simon?' she said. 'He's desperate to show you his new Ovaltiney badge and he needs help working out the secret code. He can't manage it by himself.'

'No thanks,' I said. 'I'm not that desperate.'

'He's really not that bad, you know,' Aunty Mabel tried again, but she didn't know what a nasty little worm Simon was. He was all sweetness and light when she was around, but as soon as her back was turned he was always trying to get me into trouble.

'Well, why don't you go for a walk then?' she suggested. 'You used to like walking in the woods.'

That was only when Nicholas was waiting for me at the gap in the fence. There wasn't much point now. But I decided to go anyway because Aunty Mabel was still on the "why don't you play with Simon?" warpath.

I made my way to the gap in the fence and picked up our stone, just in case there was a teensy chance that Nicholas was still here and had left me a note, but yet again my message to him was still there. Or *was* that my message? The paper looked newer. I opened it up slowly, my heart was beating fast, and ... I couldn't believe it! There was a message from Nicholas:

26 10 10 40   26 10   18 28   30 42 36

6 2 26 32   28 10 48 40   2 12 40 10 36

4 36 10 2 22 12 2 38 40

(Message No. 5)

The next Saturday

I asked Aunty Mabel if I could have a picnic lunch today.

She looked puzzled. 'It's a bit cold for a picnic, Nellie. Are you meeting someone?'

I looked innocent and shook my head. 'No, Aunty Mabel, I'm going to do a bit of my novel in the woods to get the right atmosphere.'

'Well, I suppose it's a sunny day,' she said. 'But don't be long; we've got some visitors this afternoon and I could do with a hand.'

'I won't be long,' I said happily. 'I'll help you for the rest of the day, I promise.'

Nicholas's face appeared in the gap in the fence. 'Ooh, is that strawberry jam? Thanks Eleanor, my favourite. Yummy.'

'Tell me what happened,' I demanded, handing him the biggest part of my sandwich. He munched for a bit before starting.

'I got into terrible trouble. They tried to make me tell them how I got out, but I wouldn't.'

'So what did they do to you?'

'I got six of the best.'

'What's that?' I asked.

'They hit you with a cane, like a big stick. Six times. On the backside.'
I was horrified and gave him another sandwich.

'And you still kept mum?'
He nodded proudly. 'I did. They still haven't found the gap in the fence, and they don't know about you.'

I gasped, really impressed. 'What happened next? I haven't seen you for ages. Did they lock you in the dungeons?'

He shook his head. 'They put me in detention and I had to write lots of lines, "I will not leave the school premises without permission," a hundred times. And they wrote to Mother.'

'What did she say? Was she angry?'

'I don't know,' he replied. 'I haven't heard back yet.'

'I can't believe they haven't expelled you yet,' I said.

'I know,' he replied gloomily. 'I don't know what I have to do to make them send me home. Rob a bank or something, I expect.' He jumped up. 'I've got to be off. We're going on a trip to a farm this afternoon for tea and cake. What are you up to?'

'I'm helping Aunty Mabel this afternoon.'

'I'll try and leave another message for you during the week, but I've got to be really careful now. They're watching me like a hawk and I don't want them to find the gap in the fence.'

When I got back Aunty Mabel was rolling out some scone dough. She pointed to her best tablecloth lying on a chair.

'Put that on the table for me, will you Nellie?' she said. 'And make sure you smooth it properly, no creases. And then get out

186

the nice china cups and saucers.'

'Is someone important coming?' I asked. She didn't normally go to all this trouble when visitors popped in.

'Yes,' she said. 'I've agreed to do afternoon tea for some boys who've been evacuated nearby. They're staying in the castle on the hill. I don't think you know about the castle, do you?'

I nearly dropped the saucers in surprise. The school she was talking about was Nicholas's school. Nicholas was coming here, to Sunnyvale Farm, for his afternoon tea treat!

'Steady there! I wanted you to get the crockery out, not throw it around the room!'

'Sorry Aunty Mabel, I slipped a bit,' I said, trying not to sound too excited. Aunty Mabel came and helped me get the rest of the crockery out. 'I'd like you to serve the teas when they come. Do you think you'll be able to do that without dropping anything?'

'I'll be fine Aunty Mabel, don't worry. I'll be really careful.'

It's just great having a secret friend! I can't wait to see Nicholas's face when he walks in and sees me!

He didn't notice me at first, not until they were all sitting quietly round the table, with their hands politely in their laps, and I walked over with the teapot.

'Would you like tea?' I asked loudly. He looked up at me and nearly fell off his chair with shock. It was really hard not to laugh out loud.

'Er… yes,' he stammered.
His teacher frowned. 'That's not how we speak, Nicholas,' he said. 'How about some manners?'

'Sorry, yes please miss.'

'That's better.'

'There's some milk in the jug on the table,' I said helpfully.

'Thank you miss,' Nicholas said, trying to hide a smile.

There were eleven other boys, all about the same age as Nicholas. They were quite shy at first, but after a while they began to chatter. Aunty Mabel asked them lots of questions and made them laugh with stories about the animals, but I was pleased she didn't tell them about how Hitler the rooster attacked me when I first came to the farm, or about the cow incident.
There was one very awful moment at the end of the afternoon when I thought we'd been rumbled. Just as the boys were leaving, Aunty Mabel stared straight into Nicholas's face.

'Do I know you?' she asked him. 'You look very familiar.'

'Oh no, Mrs Lammerton,' Nicholas said quickly, and went very red. 'I don't think we've met before.'

How could Aunty Mabel know Nicholas? It could only have been at the Allentide party, and I had kept him well away from her. Aunty Mabel looked at me, her eyes narrowing. 'What about you, Nellie? Does he seem familiar to you?'

'Oh no, Aunty Mabel,' I said putting a
vague expression on my face. 'I've never
seen him before in my life.'
  I'll have to be careful around Aunty Mabel
in future. She doesn't miss a trick.

WEDNESDAY When I got home from school
there was a parcel addressed
to me. I'd never had a parcel in the post
before. It was from Mum. I took off the
string and put it in my pocket in case I
needed it for something else, and then
carefully took off the brown paper.
  It was a dress. It was blue with a Peter
Pan collar. My dream dress! How did Mum
know about it, and where did she get it from?

23 Albert Gardens,
Stepney E1,
London.

Dear Nellie,
          I hope you are all well. I've put a letter for
Frank in this parcel, and some new trousers and a new
shirt.
  I hope you like the dress. Mary O'Reilly's mum brought it
round to our house and said Mary wanted you to have it
because you'd always liked it. She said you had been kind
to Mary while she was in Cornwall. She also put in some
silk stockings and a pair of Mary Jane shoes. I know you
always wanted some, I hope they fit you.

We're starting to think about Christmas now, but there's not much in the shops so I'm knitting a new balaclava each for the twins and Frank. I'm really missing you both.

George has been home on leave but he's now been posted somewhere new. He's promised to write as soon as he's settled. The bombs are still dropping here. It seems like half of London is a pile of rubble.

Our Maureen told me to tell you that she's been chosen to be the Angel Gabriel in the school nativity play. I got your lovely white dress out of the pawn shop for her to wear. The twins are playing the front and back end of the donkey. I don't know what the silly priest is thinking of, they're bound to create trouble.

From your loving
  Mum
  xxxx

I tried the dress on and it is perfect! I hugged myself in the mirror. I can't believe my dream dress is finally mine! I look like a film star! The shoes are a bit tight but Uncle Ray says that he will have a go at stretching them for me.

'That's given me an idea for a nice Christmas present for your families, children,' Aunty Mabel said at the supper table. 'We could have a trip into town and pay a visit to the photographer there, and have your photographs taken.'

It sounded really exciting. Not only have I got the most beautiful dress ever, I'm being photographed wearing it! Yippee!

SATURDAY Morning:
It rained during the night but the sun is shining and a few white, puffy clouds are hovering in the sky.
Last night Aunty Mabel put my hair in curlers to make me pretty for the photograph, so I'm hoping that she has more luck than Mum and Jean ever did. My lovely dress is laid over the chair waiting for me to put it on and Uncle Ray has stretched my shoes so that they only pinch my toes a tiny bit. My stockings are washed, ready.

I can hear Aunty Mabel downstairs getting ready for breakfast so I'd better get up and give her a hand. I'll have a wash first and put my stockings on ready, but I'll put my old clothes on just in case I have an accident and get my lovely dress dirty.

'Can you go and get the eggs please Nellie?' Aunty Mabel handed me the basket as I went into the kitchen. Oh blast, that meant I had to tackle Hitler.

'Oh, can't Simon do it today, Aunty Mabel?' I whined. 'I don't want to get dirty.'

'No,' she replied firmly. 'Simon's taking the cows to the field with Frank. You've got the easy job this morning Nellie, now get to it please.'

Hitler was in a foul mood this morning.
I'd hardly got through the gate before he
came at me. I swung the basket at him but it
only stopped him for a moment. As he charged
at me again, I ran back out through the gate,
slamming it shut behind me. I shuddered. He
was so horrible. What was I going to do?

'You're going to have to get the better of
him eventually,' said a voice. Phew, it was
Uncle Ray.

'Yes, but please don't make it today, Uncle
Ray,' I said. 'I'm all smart, ready for the
photo. What will Aunty Mabel say if I get
all dirty?'
He smiled. 'All right then, I'll get them.
Pass me the basket.'

I watched while Uncle Ray did his strange
dance with Hitler, and then once the rooster
had been "moved" out of the way, Uncle Ray
disappeared into the hen house and came out
with a basket full of lovely brown eggs.

I have to come clean now and tell you that
this actually happened every day. Although
it was my job to collect the eggs, it was
really Uncle Ray who did it every morning.
Aunty Mabel didn't know that though.

'There you go then Nellie,' said Uncle Ray
as he passed me the basket.

'Remember, it's just our little secret,
Uncle Ray,' I said.

'But you'll have to do it tomorrow,' he said. 'You can't rely on me to be here every day to rescue you.' He always says that, but he hasn't let me down yet.

Late Morning:

I'm ready to go. My dress and ribbon are exactly the same shade of blue. My silk stockings fit perfectly and my Mary Janes are sparkling. My hair has curled properly for the first time ever. I look a million dollars.

Frank and Simon are downstairs waiting, looking incredibly smart, even I have to admit that.

'Come on Cinderella,' said Uncle Ray, bowing low and sweeping his arm gracefully. 'Your carriage awaits. Time to go to the ball.' I giggled and took his arm.

There wasn't far to go across the muddy farmyard. Aunty Mabel was waiting in the truck and the boys were in the back. I was to sit between her and Uncle Ray at the front. Just a few teeny, tiny delicate steps in my Mary Janes and I would be safe and dry, sitting next to her.

But suddenly there was a gleeful, "Woof, woof, woof!" and Flossie came flying round the side of the house. She leapt towards me excitedly, her enormous muddy paws coming straight for me. All I managed to do was turn away from her slightly before she leapt at me.

'Oh no!' I thought as I felt my feet leave the ground. It seemed to take hours as I flew through the air - and then my bottom landed SPLAT! Right into the largest muddy puddle in the farmyard.

'Get up Nellie!' Aunty Mabel shrieked at me as if I'd gone for a swim in the puddle on purpose.

'Who let that wretched dog out?' Uncle Ray was shouting furiously. Simon looked a bit guilty but didn't say anything. Aunty Mabel pulled me out of the mud.

'Stop crying, Nellie,' she said and she sponged down my lovely ruined dress as best as she could. 'The mud's only on the back, it won't show in the photograph.'

Uncle Ray cleaned my Mary Janes. I was still crying. My stockings were filthy and couldn't be worn. Aunty Mabel disappeared and came back with a pair of Frank's enormous, long woolly grey socks.

'You'll have to put these on,' she said. They were really itchy and awful and they made my shoes feel even tighter.

'For goodness sake, stop that grizzling,' said Aunty Mabel. 'You'll make your face all ugly for the photograph. What will your mother think?'

Here is the photograph:

  My hair's gone a bit wild, and those awful socks, YUK! But actually, I'm pretty pleased with the result. You can't see the mud on my dress, thank goodness.

I know Mum will love it.

Even though I miss my mum, I've got used to life on the farm. I'm treated really well, Frank is fit and healthy again, and even Simon has stopped following me around because he has Frank to annoy now. I'm pretty lucky compared to some children, I know.

So why, oh why did I spoil everything?

One of the nearby farms has been turned into a prisoner of war camp where they keep the German prisoners of war. We've been told by Mr Martin *and* by Aunty Mabel, under no circumstances should we go near the place, so of course Nicholas and I sneaked round to have a look once.

We saw some men working in the fields around the camp but they didn't look much like prisoners; they were smiling and laughing with each other.

'I don't think they can be the prisoners,' I said to Nicholas. 'I expect the prisoners are chained up, or locked in rooms with bars at the door.'

Nicholas nodded in agreement. 'They look too ordinary to be Germans,' he said.

Today, I was walking back from school by myself when the church bell in the village square rang. People came out of their homes

197

to see what was happening because the bells only usually rang on Sunday mornings before church.

The Home Guard came marching through the village square and lined up in straight rows, their guns upright on their shoulders. The Home Guard were some of the local men who weren't fighting in the war, but they were soldiers in their spare time.

I stopped to watch what was going on.

'Atten–SHUN!' shouted the soldier in charge.

They all stamped their feet at the same time.

'Now listen men, we have an escaped German prisoner. It's unlikely he's got too far. We need to find him quickly. He may well be armed and dangerous, so be prepared to shoot on sight if he doesn't surrender.'
An excited buzz went through the crowd of villagers who had gathered. The man looked over at us.

'All children need to get home as quickly as possible. As for the rest of you, get into your homes and lock your doors. This is a dangerous and desperate man.'

One lady shrieked with horror and looked like she was about to faint.

'Gather your children and keep yourselves safe. I don't want anybody trying to be a hero. Let me and my men deal with this. We're highly trained to deal with these situations.'

I ran off home, my heart thumping with excitement. There was a real German on the loose!

I just got into the kitchen when Frank came charging in, out of breath.

'Have you heard about the escaped prisoner? I'm helping Uncle Ray and his men search for him. Jam tarts? Yum. I'll have two of those. Lock the door, Nellie, and keep safe.' And then he was gone, banging the door behind him.

As if I was going to take orders from him! I called out for Aunty Mabel but she didn't seem to be around, which was unusual because she was always in the kitchen when we got home from school.

Then I suddenly had a frightening thought. What if she'd been captured by the German prisoner and was being held hostage? I decided to have a look around and see if I could find her. I needed a weapon just in case I had to tackle him and rescue Aunty Mabel. Then I spotted the rolling pin on the

draining board. Just the thing. I crept
through the house, slowly opening all the
doors before calling, 'Aunty Mabel, are you
in here?' but there was no answer. I looked
through the window in my attic room and saw
Uncle Ray, Frank and the farm workers heading
towards the top field in search of the
prisoner. They looked just like the Home
Guard marching across the field, but instead
of guns they carried spades and pitchforks on
their shoulders.

I went outside and had a quick look in the
hen house. She wasn't there either. The only
place left to look was the cow shed, which I
wasn't too keen on because of the smell. But
I needed to be brave - Aunty Mabel could be
in danger! Holding my nose, I opened the
door and went inside.

'Aunty Mabel?'
No answer, apart from Beamish giving me a
'hello' moo.

Just as I was about
to shut the door, a
tiny movement in the
hayloft caught my
eye. I had a strange
feeling that someone
was in there. I
decided to play a

trick on whoever it was. I shouted loudly,
'Bye, Beamish, bye, Avis, Mavis, Dolly, Rita
and Talulah!' as if I was leaving, but

instead of going out I closed the door with a big bang and ran behind a box near Beamish's stall. I crouched down with my heart thumping and waited, wishing Nicholas was with me.

Suddenly the hay in the hay loft started moving and rustling and a man dressed like a farm worker emerged from the hay. I breathed a sigh of relief. It wasn't the German prisoner - it was probably one of Uncle Ray's men having a sneaky snooze. I watched as he came down the loft ladder and noticed that his trousers were ripped and his leg was bleeding. I came out from behind Beamish's box and went towards him.

'Hello,' I said. 'If you're looking for Uncle Ray, he's gone up to the top field with the others, looking for the escaped German. You've cut yourself, did you realise?' The man jumped when he saw me and looked terrified.

'It's all right. I won't tell Uncle Ray you were asleep in here, don't worry.' I pointed to his leg. 'Aunty Mabel could put a bandage on that if you like. You don't want it going septic.'
He didn't speak, and he still look frightened. Then I began to get frightened too. What if he wasn't one of Uncle Ray's farm workers, what if he was ... *the escaped prisoner!*

Then he spoke: 'Don't be afraid, little girl, I won't harm you.' He spoke English with a strange accent. He wasn't Cornish, or a Londoner. In fact, he didn't sound English at all.

'Are you him? The German prisoner?' I asked, sounding braver than I felt.
He nodded. 'Please don't be afraid,' he said again.

I don't know what I expected a German to look like. A bit like a baddie in the Westerns, I suppose, with thick, dark eyebrows and a twirly moustache. The prisoner had ordinary light brown hair and blue eyes. He didn't look at all scary, just tired and a bit sad.

'Why are you trying to escape?' I asked. 'Did they treat you badly in the prison camp?'
He sat down wearily and shook his head. 'No no, they treat us very well. I get to work outside in the fields, which I enjoy.' He put his hand into his pocket and slowly took

 out an old photograph. It was a bit bent on the corners. He carefully straightened them and handed it to me. It was a picture of a pretty

blonde lady and a little girl about my age. They were both smiling.

'This is my wife Anna, and my daughter Helga. I'm trying to get home to Germany so that I can see them. I miss them very much.'

'I miss my dad,' I told him. 'He's fighting the Germ -, he's away at the moment.' I felt a bit awkward talking about it. I looked at the picture again. 'Is your daughter evacuated?'

He shook his head. 'No, she is with my wife in Hamburg. I'm worried that they will be hit by a bomb. I want to get them away into the countryside. War is a terrible thing. It makes enemies of people who were once friends.'

I felt confused. I didn't like to think of my dad and George hurting other people like Anna and Helga while they were fighting in the war. I'm sure they didn't.

The German looked towards the door. 'Well, what's going to happen next? Are you going to tell your aunty I'm here, or will you let me go?'

I didn't know what to do. I looked at his leg.

'You won't be able to run very fast with all that bleeding.'

He smiled sadly. 'No, I won't,' he said. 'You are quite right.'

'How did you hurt it?'

'I caught it on some barbed wire when I was climbing over the fence.'

I began to think about my own dad. What if *he* was trying to escape from somewhere and a little girl found him. What would I want her to do? Tell on him, or help him?

Surely it wouldn't be wrong to help him. He just wanted to go home and look after his family.

'Wait here,' I told him. 'I'll go and get you a bandage for your leg.'

'Thank you,' he smiled his sad smile and closed his eyes.

I rushed inside to the kitchen and found the bandages in a drawer in the dresser. Then I cut a piece of the chicken and ham pie Aunty Mabel had made for supper and wrapped it in a napkin. I put them both into my pocket and went back into the cowshed.

'You are very kind,' said the German. While I wrapped the bandage round his leg he told me a bit about himself.

'When I was younger I went to Oxford University in England. I made many friends while I was there. One of them lives in Devon. I am trying to make my way to their house and hope they will help me get back to Germany.'

'It's probably best if you don't tell me too much, then I won't have to fib as much if I'm asked any questions.'

'Quite so,' he said. 'I forgot myself there for a moment. I'm feeling quite dizzy. I think it's the loss of blood.'

When he was ready to leave I reached into my pocket and gave him the pie. He smiled and took it. 'May I ask your name?' he said.

'I'm called Nellie,' I told him.

'My name is Peter. Peter Schmidt.' He saluted to me. 'Thank you little Nellie. I look forward to the day this war will end and our countries will be at peace again. I will never forget the little English girl who helped a wounded German prisoner.'

'I hope you find your wife and Helga.' I told him. 'Hang about here, I'll just see if the coast is clear before you go,' and stuck my head out of the door. To my horror, who should be in the yard but Simon.

'What are you doing in the cowshed Nellie?' he said.

'Nothing, just checking on Beamish and Avis.'

'Why? You don't normally. And why are you looking so suspicious?'

'I'm not.'

'You are. Are you hiding something?'

'No, just shove off, will you?'

'Let me have a look then. Gerroff my arm Nellie. What's the matter with you? Oh blimey! It's the escaped prisoner! HELP! HELP! UNCLE RAY, THE PRISONER'S IN HERE!'

Before I could do anything, loads of men had swarmed into the cowshed and grabbed hold of Peter. They pulled him out by his arms, and his feet were being dragged along the ground. I couldn't bear to see him taken away back to prison and never get to see his family again. I ran back into the kitchen.

The door opened and Simon came in. 'They've got him,' he said joyfully. 'They've got your horrible German, Nellie, and they're taking him back to the prison camp.'

'He's not my German,' I said.

'I can't believe you were trying to help a German escape. You're really for it, Nellie Walker. You're a traitor and do you know what they do with traitors? They lock 'em up in the Tower of London, or they shoot 'em.'

At that moment Aunty Mabel came in, panting heavily. She'd been running.

'I went down to the school to collect you because I didn't want you walking by yourselves with the prisoner on the loose,' she said. 'And then he's found in our own cowshed. Who would have thought it?'

'And who would have thought Nellie would be a traitor to her King and country?' Simon smirked. I wish I could have slapped his face. Twice.

Aunty Mabel frowned at him.

'Be quiet, Simon. Get off to bed, both of you,' she said.

'But it's still early and we haven't had anything to eat,' Simon whined. 'And I didn't do anything wrong, it was Nellie!'

'Take a piece of pie with you, both of you.' She looked tired and upset. 'Nellie, get upstairs before Frank comes in with the men. I couldn't cope with an argument right now.'

So I'm sitting on my bed. My pie is still on the little table next to me. I can't eat it because I feel sick in my stomach. What's going to happen to me? Am I going to be arrested and taken away? What will Mum and Dad think when they find out?

THURSDAY Today was the most horrible day of my life. When I came down to breakfast Aunty Mabel wasn't in a good mood.

'Take your snack, Nellie, and get to school.'

'Shall I wait for Frank?'

'No, get yourself off now. Frank's going in a bit later.'

'Why?'

'Because I don't want to walk with you,' said a voice. It was Frank coming into the kitchen. 'I'm ashamed of you.'

'That's enough of that, Frank.' Aunty Mabel said.

I felt tears sting my eyes and I had an enormous lump in my throat.

'I can't believe you were trying to help a German prisoner escape,' Frank said. 'Did you think about what would have happened if he got back to Germany?'

'He was worried about his family,' I said. 'He wanted to rescue them.'

'They would have sent him straight back to war, Nellie,' Frank shouted. 'Back to killing Dad, or George or dropping bombs on our mum!'

'He wasn't evil, or anything like I imagined a German would be,' I whispered. 'He's just somebody's dad. He's got a little girl about my age. I saw her photo and she didn't look wicked. She looked really nice.'

'She's not nice, she's the enemy!' Frank shouted again.

'Stop it now, Frank,' Aunty Mabel said firmly. 'You forget that Nellie is only little. I'll be glad when this war is over and we're all at peace again.'

'That's what he said,' I told her. 'I just don't understand what's going on. The world is a horrible place.' I was trying not to cry.

'Get to school now before Simon comes down,' Aunty Mabel held out my coat. 'You know what he's like.'

Simon was much worse than I could have imagined. As soon as he got to school he told everyone what had happened. He had a crowd round him listening to every word he said. He was really enjoying himself because normally nobody ever spoke to him.

When I got into the classroom, nobody would sit next to me. They whispered and sniggered. Somebody kept firing paper balls at the back of my head. Mr Martin kept giving me nasty looks, but other than that he ignored me all day, which actually I was pleased about.

At lunchtime I sat by myself in the corner of the playground. Rosie came over to me. 'You're disgusting, Nellie Walker. You shouldn't be here with decent people.' And then she slapped me round the face, really hard. I didn't say anything, but I didn't cry either. Everybody laughed and called me names like, "German lover" and "stinky traitor."

I don't know how I got through the rest of the afternoon. It was even worse than the morning, but eventually the bell went and I decided to go to the gap in the fence and leave a message for Nicholas. I didn't write it in code, I wasn't in the mood.

I've done a terrible thing. I tried to help a German prisoner escape and now I'm a traitor. I might be arrested and shot so I'm running away back to London. I'll be here before it gets light tomorrow morning. If you still want to be my friend, please meet me. If not I will understand. Everything is so awful.

FRIDAY Early:

Everybody's still asleep.
I've packed my knapsack and taken a piece of pie. I've written a note for Aunty Mabel:

Dear Aunty Mabel and Uncle Ray,
thank you for looking after me so well.
I've had such a nice time. I'm running away because I don't want to be shot as a traitor. I'm sorry I've let you down.
Love Nellie xxx

In the
kitchen,
Flossie was
lying by the
stove to
keep warm.
She whined
and
her tail
banged

against the floor when she saw me. I gave
her a big cuddle and she licked the tears
from my cheek. 'Goodbye Flossie, I love
you,' I whispered.

I took another piece of pie from the
larder, grabbed my coat and hat, shut the
back door and made my way towards the gap in
the fence. It had started to snow.

Nicholas was waiting for me. He had a bag
next to him. 'I'm coming with you,' he said.
'Let's get going before it gets light. You
can tell me what happened on the way.'
I started to cry again. I never imagined
that he would come with me.

Nicholas had stolen lots of food from the
school kitchen to keep us going.
'I think we should head for the train
station,' he said. 'There's an early train to
London we could catch before anyone's
realised we're gone.'

'How did you find that out?'

'I went into the headmaster's study and found a train timetable in his desk drawer.' I just can't believe how brave and fearless Nicholas is.

'Have you got any train fare?' I said. "I haven't got any money. I was just going to get on the train and hide in the lav.'

'Don't worry,' he said. 'Mother sent me some for Christmas just in case something happened and she couldn't get down to visit me. We can buy the tickets with that.'

As we walked, the snow came down harder. I told Nicholas everything that had happened.

'Do you still want to know me?' I asked him when I had finished. 'I'll understand if you want to go back.'

'Of course I don't want to go back,' Nicholas replied. 'You did what you thought was right. I know you did it for the little girl so that she could have her father back. You weren't trying to lose the war for England or anything.'

I gave Nicholas an enormous smile. He *is* the best friend ever.

By the time we got to the station it was almost daylight, but we couldn't see much in front of us because the snow was falling so thickly. The door to the waiting room was locked so we had to sit outside on a bench.

'I wonder what the time is?' I said. 'Do you think we might have missed the train?'

'Don't worry,' Nicholas said. 'If we have, there'll be another one along soon.'

We waited and waited but no train came. The station master didn't appear either. We began to feel really cold. I was shivering all over.

'We need to move about otherwise we'll freeze to death,' I said, so we kicked the snow and did silly dances. Then we made snowballs and threw them at each other. We had a great time.

'We'd better have some breakfast,' Nicholas said, getting some bread and jam out of his bag.

'Ooh lovely, strawberry!'

We were munching away when we noticed the station master opening the door to the waiting room.

'Have we missed the early train?' Nicholas asked him.

The station master shook his head. 'No,' he said. 'This weather's delayed all the trains. They'll be trying to get the snow off the line. I've got to do the same here. I'm expecting some help from the Home Guard in a minute.' Nicholas and I looked at each other in horror. The Home Guard were the last people we wanted to see. They'd arrest me for sure. And they might even arrest Nicholas for helping a traitor!

'Anyway, where are you two off to?'

'We're going back to London,' I said. 'Our parents are really missing us and they've asked us to come home.' Only half a fib.

'But I suppose we'd better get back to our house if there isn't going to be a train,' (a whole fib). 'Cheerio then.' And we ran as fast as we could through the snow.

'Where are we going?' I panted next to him.

'We'll have to try and make it to the next village and wait for the train from there,' Nicholas said.

'But that's miles away!'

'Have you got a better idea?' But I hadn't so we set off down what we thought might be the road.

Afternoon: It had finally stopped snowing and the sun was shining. It bounced off the snow into our eyes, almost blinding us. The whole world had turned white. It was really beautiful, like a real-life Christmas card, but it made it really difficult to recognise where we were — everywhere looked the same.

'I think we're lost,' I said eventually. We'd been walking for hours.

Nicholas nodded in agreement. 'I think you're right.'

'What shall we do?'

'Have something to eat.'

Nicholas spotted some trees in the distance. 'I think that might be the woods near my school, Nellie. Let's make for there!'

It took us a lot longer than we thought to reach the woods, but when we arrived we didn't recognise it.

'We could be anywhere!' I said.

'But at least it's more sheltered in here,' said Nicholas. 'We're out of that awful wind now.'

We walked further and deeper into the woods, but we didn't see a soul. Then eventually, in between a clump of trees, I saw what looked like a shelter. It was built with large branches, roughly put together like a small, wonky Indian tepee, and someone had made a door with a dirty piece of cloth. It looked abandoned.

'Let's shelter in there,' I said.

We stepped closer and closer to the door.
I raised my hand to lift back the curtain
when suddenly it was wrenched to one side and
a menacingly, familiar face loomed out at me.
It was a woman, as big as a man and as wide
as a door, with long, matted black hair and a
face as ugly as the devil.

'Sally Nightshade!' I screamed. A big,
gnarly hand shot out and grabbed me by the
arm.

'Pesky kids!' she roared. 'They've ruined
me! Was it you? Was it you that ruined me?'
She shook me so hard, I thought my eyes were
going to fall out.

'Leave her alone!' Nicholas was shouting
and hitting her at the same time. 'Let her
go, you old cow!' Then he took an enormous,
savage bite out of her arm.

'Aaaaarrrrhhhh!' she screamed, dropping me
onto the ground.

'Run, Nellie, run for your life!' Nicholas roared at me. He pulled me up and we ran and ran through the thick snow, not daring to look back and see if she was following.

We were back out of the woods before we finally stopped. Nicholas was bent double, trying to get his breath back.

'Is she behind us?' he wheezed.

'I don't think so,' I panted. 'I can't see her.' I looked behind us, but we seemed to be safe.

'Which way do you think we should go now?'

'That way,' I pointed towards some white, snowy hills. I didn't have a clue where to go, or what to do really, but we had to walk somewhere. We were soaking wet and freezing and I couldn't feel my feet.

'Why don't we have something to eat while we're walking?' I said, although I didn't have anything myself.

I watched Nicholas as he ate. His hands and face were bright red with cold and he couldn't stop shivering. I felt really guilty. I was the one in trouble and I'd dragged poor Nicholas into this mess with me.

'I think we should go back, Nicholas,' I decided. 'We're completely lost and we've almost run out of food. We could be walking for days.'

'But you might be shot if we go back!'

'At least this way you'll be safe. We'll go back to Torwenno and I'll give myself up to the Home Guard.'

'But we don't know the way back to Torwenno,'

'True,' I sighed. 'We may as well keep going this way.'

Later: It began to get dark. We'd been walking nearly all day. The snow was falling again and we couldn't see through the blizzard. Nicholas was turning blue and he'd been having trouble breathing since we'd run out of the woods. Suddenly he stumbled and fell into the snow, and he lay there with his eyes closed.

'Get up, get up!' I shouted, horrified. I tried to pull him up but he was too heavy. I sat down on the cold, wet snow and pulled him on my lap to keep him dry.

'I'm so sorry, Nicholas,' I sobbed. 'We're going to die and it's all my fault!'

Just then I heard a rumbling sound that made the ground shake. It was getting nearer and nearer. It sounded like an earthquake. We were definitely done for now. I closed my eyes and said my prayers.

When I opened my eyes I couldn't believe what
I was seeing! In the dim light I could just
about see what looked like a long line of
tractors all making their way across the snow
towards us. As
they got closer
I could see
Uncle Ray's face
over Blue
Bessie's
steering wheel.
Flossie was next
to him, barking
and barking. I
stood up and
began to wave my
arms madly. 'We're here, Uncle Ray! We're
here!' Then my head went all dizzy and
everything went black.

Night time: We were in the sitting room at
Sunnyvale Farm. I was on the sofa, wrapped
in blankets next to a roaring fire, drinking
tea. Nicholas was snuggled next to me,
tucking into a large piece of Aunty Mabel's
apple cake. He'd already eaten three
pasties.   Flossie had her chin on my lap.

Frank was sitting on the floor at my feet. Uncle Ray was perched on the sofa arm close to me, and kept patting my head from time to time. Aunty Mabel was constantly in and out with more food.

'I'm having trouble keeping up with you lot,' she said, carrying in another tray of pasties. 'My poor old stove thinks it's cooking for an army!'

When our stomachs were finally full, Uncle Ray began to speak.

'You gave us a terrible fright, running away, Nellie,' he said.

'I'm so sorry,' I could feel myself blushing. 'I was frightened I was going to be shot as a traitor.'

Uncle Ray sighed. 'No-one's going to shoot you, or do anything else to you, Nellie - you're just a child. We don't do that sort of thing in England. Everybody was worried about you. You saw how many people were out looking for you!'

'The poor child didn't know that,' Aunty Mabel said. 'I'm sorry Nellie, we've let you down. You shouldn't have been left here by yourself at such a dangerous time.'

'But I wasn't in any danger, Peter was a nice man. He was just trying to get home to look after his family.'

Uncle Ray nodded. 'Luckily for you. The British officers at the POW camp said that he was a peaceful man and had caused them no trouble, other than escaping, of course. He was part of a crew of a U-boat that our boys had sunk. He'll be treated well, but he won't see his family again until after the war. That's if they're still alive.' I felt so sad for him.

'Why do we have to have this stupid war? *We* don't want the war, and I can't believe that all the Germans want it either. Peter certainly didn't.'

Uncle Ray sighed. 'I can't pretend to know what it's all about, Nellie. All I know is that Adolph Hitler wants to rule the world, and there are plenty of people who support him. We have to stop him, and that's about as far as my knowledge of the whole thing goes. But what I do know is, one day this war will be over, and everything will be peaceful again, and it'll be people like you, Nellie, who will lead the way. People who are kind and don't judge others.'

'I'm flabbergasted!' I said.

'Why?' asked Uncle Ray.

'I've never heard you speak so much before, Uncle Ray!'

'Where's *you know who*, by the way?' I
asked, realising Simon wasn't hanging around,
as usual.

'Simon's not here tonight,' Aunty Mabel
said. 'Rosie's parents have agreed to take
him in for a couple of days. I understand
they've become quite good friends.'

'We thought it might be a good idea, just
until things have calmed down a bit,' said
Uncle Ray. 'But this constant arguing between
the two of you needs to stop, Nellie. It's
bad enough being at war with Germany, without
having another war in the house.'

'But it's not me, It's him!' I said.

'Is it?' said Aunty Mabel gently. 'I've
noticed quite a few times that Simon's tried
to be friends with you and you haven't
exactly been very nice to him.'

I sat for a while and thought about it.
Actually, I have to admit, I do remember
Simon trying to be friends with me when we
first started school in the village, and
wanting to be an Ovaltiney so that we could
send messages to each other. *And* trying to
play with me lots of times, but I was always
in a hurry to run off and be with Nicholas.

'I suppose I haven't been very nice to him
really,' I admitted grudgingly. 'I can sort
of understand why he tries to get me into
trouble — to get back at me for not wanting
to play with him.'

222

'That's very mature of you to see things like that, Nellie,' said Aunty Mabel. 'I'm very proud of you.'

'Do you think I should talk to him?' I said. I didn't want to really, particularly because Simon had been so horrible to me last time I saw him, but I owed it to Aunty Mable and Uncle Ray to stop the squabbling. 'Should I go to Rosie's house and see him?'

'I don't think so,' said Uncle Ray. 'It won't do him any harm to ponder on things for a few days. Even though you could have been nicer to him, he's behaved pretty badly in all of this.'

'Uncle Ray gave him a huge telling off,' said Frank. 'Both of us, actually.' He looked down, ashamed. 'I'm sorry I didn't stick up for you Nellie, I promise I'll never let you down again.'

I couldn't believe what I was hearing! Everything had been turned around. I wasn't a traitor anymore! I was a kind person – a leader of the future! Perhaps I might even be Prime Minister one day!

'And besides,' said Aunty Mabel cheerfully. 'We need the bed for another guest until the snow clears.'

'Is that me?" Nicholas squeaked excitedly.

The doctor had been with Uncle Ray on the rescue mission. He'd examined both of us and said that Nicholas had Bronchitis in his chest, and needed lots of rest and warmth. As the weather was so bad, and the roads were closed, Aunty Mabel had offered to look after him at Sunnyvale Farm until he was feeling better.

'You're turning into a really good nurse, Aunty Mabel.' I said. 'What with Frank, and now Nicholas.'

Of course, Nicholas and I had had to explain to Aunty Mabel and Uncle Ray about our secret friendship. They laughed out loud when we told them the story about Nicholas dressing up in my clothes to come to the Allentide party.

'I knew I recognised you from somewhere,' Aunty Mabel said to Nicholas. 'Even if you were dressed as a girl at the time!'

After that everyone went to bed. Aunty Mabel let Nicholas and me camp down in the sitting room in front of the fire. We snuggled up in our blankets and stared into the dancing flames.

'We've had a real-life adventure, Eleanor,' Nicholas said excitedly. 'We've been plucked from the jaws of death and survived to tell the tale.'

'If that's what an adventure is like,' I groaned, that's the last one I'm having. *Ever!*

SUNDAY We've had even more snow. Frank made a big grinning snowman in the front garden and it peered through the window at us. Nicholas and I stayed by the fire in the sitting room and mostly played Ludo and card games. Sometimes I wrote a bit of my novel, and then read it to Nicholas. He liked the bit when Tex rescued Bella and they were caught by the baddies while he was untying her.

Desert Hero continued ...

"Where do you think you're going?" said a sneering voice. Tex spun round to see Mad Man standing there with his gun in his hand.

"Get your hands in the air, you cowardly dog!" Mad Man shouted at Tex.

"We're done for, Tex," Bella breathed.

MONDAY Bad news. The tractors cleared the lane from the farm to the village today and because Nicholas was feeling stronger, a car came from the school to take him back. He wasn't well enough to go to lessons so he would stay in the school hospital, which they called the *Sanatorium*.

PC Trescott came to visit with news about Mad Sally Nightshade. She had been found in the woods and arrested. Apparently, she very quickly blabbed and told the police who else was involved in her black-market meat gang. They had all been caught and taken away to prison in Truro, our nearest large town. Frank was really relieved. He hadn't been able to settle properly while she was still at large, and he was always half expecting her to come looking for him. Now he could finally relax and forget about the whole horrible business.

TUESDAY Simon came back to Sunnyvale farm this afternoon looking very awkward and embarrassed. I decided not to make a fuss about it and just asked him very casually if he wanted to play Ludo. He seemed really relieved. I nearly let him win at one point, but I changed my mind and thrashed him instead. He didn't whinge for a change.

WEDNESDAY We went back to school today because the snow had almost gone. Aunty Mabel gave us a lift in the trap.

'Do you want to sit in the front with me, Nellie?' Aunty Mabel asked. 'And the boys can go in the back.'

'No, it's all right, Aunty Mabel,' I said. 'Simon can if he wants to — I always sit in the front.'

'Actually, I'd rather sit at the back with you, Nellie,' Simon said shyly.

'Great, it'll be me at the front then,' Frank said happily, jumping up next to Aunty Mabel.

TUESDAY Things are pretty much back to normal at school now. Everybody has stopped picking on me. Simon plays with Rosie at playtime and I mostly hang around with Frank and Paddy. We're breaking up for Christmas at the end of the week, so we're spending a lot of time learning Christmas carols for the church service on Christmas day.

Even though I know Christmas at Sunnyvale Farm will be extra marvellous, I'm not particularly excited about it because Mum won't be there. I haven't heard from her for a while, even though I've written to her twice. Frank and I have had a Christmas card from George, and another one from Jean. I've even had one from Sarah, even though she's Jewish and they don't believe in Christmas. Why haven't we had a card from Mum?

This morning Aunty Mabel grabbed me as I was about to go into the yard with the egg basket. She pointed to a chair and I sat down.

'You've been such a brave girl lately,' she said. 'You've certainly shown that you won't let yourself be pushed around by anyone or anything.'
I couldn't work out what she was getting at so I said nothing and waited for her to carry on. Grown-ups do get to the point eventually.

'Or is there something that's still getting the better of you, Nellie?'

'I don't know what you're on about, Aunty Mabel,' I said, baffled.

'The game's up, Nellie,' said Uncle Ray coming into the kitchen. 'She knows that I've been getting the eggs for you.'

'For how long?' I asked.

'Right from the word go,' Aunty Mabel said and folded her arms in a determined way. 'And now it's going to stop. Nellie, today is the day you get the better of the old rooster.'

Hitler looked as if he had other ideas. I could see it in his beady little eyes as he stared, unblinking, at me. He was definitely up for a fight - but so was I. I was a different person to the little girl who had

228

first arrived in Torwenno. Aunty Mabel was right - I was brave, confident, fearless! Today was the day that I would finally defeat Hitler.

'Don't mess with me, mate,' I warned him loudly as he took a step towards me. I gulped and moved slowly towards the hen house. He took another step. He didn't take his eyes off me. We stood, barely six feet apart, looking at each other, daring the other to look away first. Then suddenly he lunged, but this time I was ready for him. I put my foot gently under Hitler's bottom and very firmly I raised my leg in the same slow kicking action, just like Uncle Ray does.

Hitler looked a bit surprised as he went flying backwards across the farmyard, but he soon recovered and came charging back at me. I did the same thing again, this time, even more expertly.

'Take that, you twerp!' I shouted. He flew backwards again and then he just stood staring at me, making a quiet clucking sound.

He didn't charge again. He knew he was beaten.

I punched the air and screamed, 'It's a howling victory for Eleanor Walker, queen of the hen house!' and I jumped up and down in a wild victory dance. I had finally got the better of Hitler! Hip hip hooray!

As I walked back towards the house with my basket full of eggs, Uncle Ray was waiting for me by the back door. 'Good for you, Nellie,' he smiled. 'Perhaps we should send you out to France to sort out the other Hitler!'

DESERT HERO cont...

Suddenly there was shouting and punching, and Mad Man McBlaine's men began to fall like skittles. It was the sheriff and his men. They guessed what Tex had done and followed him . When the rest of the baddies realised they were outnumbered they got on their horses and made for the exit.

"Let's skidaddle out of here," they said.

Mad Man turned his head to see what was happening and Tex seized his chance. He jumped on Mad Man and wrestled the gun out of his hands. Tex finished the job with a punch on Mad Man's jaw.

"So much for your men," Tex said. "Real friends don't run when the going gets tough. They stick around and fight for each other!"

**SUNDAY** (The last one before
Christmas day)

        We spent a brilliant day putting
up an enormous Christmas tree in the sitting
room. Frank and I made paper chains for the
ceiling, and Aunty Mabel baked some
decorations for the tree.

Aunty Mabel has a beautiful fairy for the top
of the tree. She has a lovely face with
bright blue eyes and rosy red cheeks, and her
hair is in a neat little dark brown bun,
sitting on the back of her neck, just like my
mum wears hers.
 'I'll call you Jane, after my mum,' I
whispered to her. I was allowed to put Jane
on the top of the tree.
  'It's tradition in our family that the
youngest puts the fairy in place,' Aunty
Mabel told us, although I don't think Frank
and Simon wanted to do it anyway.

The postman brought me a letter from Nicholas. I haven't seen him since he left Sunnyvale farm. He was still quite poorly then, and the doctor said he would be in bed for a while.

Langford House
Torwenno

Dear Eleanor,

I hope you are well, and also Frank, Simon and Mr and Mrs Lammerton.

I am feeling much better, although I am still in the sanatorium, but guess who came to see me? My mother! What a marvellous surprise!

I haven't been expelled after running away. I was pretty gutted at first, until I heard the most wonderful news - my mother is to live in my school and be our new house mother! That means I will see her every day. She'll also look after the other boys in my house and they will be so pleased because she is the most wonderful and caring mother.

We are having a special tea on Christmas Eve and everyone is allowed to invite a guest. Would you like to be my guest? It is at 3.15 pm.

Yours sincerely,
Nicholas

Christmas Eve

Morning:

I woke up and found Aunty Mable in the kitchen already cooking like a mad woman.

There were already forty-eight mince pies cooling down on the table.

'Can I have one for breakfast?' I asked her.

'Leave them be,' she said. 'They're for tomorrow.'

'But surely we won't eat that many? You've already made two Christmas puddings and an enormous Christmas cake.'

'You never know who might turn up for dinner,' she said mysteriously. 'Grab a cloth and dry some of these pans up. I need to get your hair done for your tea party later.'

Yes, can you believe it? Aunty Mabel had decided to have another go at curling my hair. I slept all night with rags in my hair and my head really hurts.

Afternoon:

I am wearing my favourite blue dress and Aunty Mabel has given me a white woollen cardigan to wear over the top.

'You make sure you don't get these clothes dirty,' she said buttoning me into the cardigan. 'They'll have to do you for tomorrow as well.' She seemed a bit flustered

233

and pink in the face. I wondered if it was because I was going for a posh tea at the castle.

'I promise I won't fall into any mud this time, Aunty Mabel,' I said laughing.

Uncle Ray gave me a lift to the school in the cart, beautifully pulled by Ned.

'I'll be back to collect you at midnight, Cinders,' he said dramatically, sweeping into a low bow at the bottom of the steps. 'We don't want you turning into a pumpkin.'

Honestly, he's really daft sometimes. 'Six o'clock will do, Uncle Ray,' I laughed.

I did feel a bit like Cinderella walking up those grand steps towards the entrance of the school, which really was a castle. The garden seemed as big as the whole of London and there was an enormous lake that Nicholas had told me they were allowed to swim in during the summer.

The large oak door was opened by an old
wrinkled lady who looked vaguely familiar.

'I'm Eleanor Jane Walker,' I told her. 'And
I've come to visit Nicholas Worthington.'
(This is what Aunty Mabel had told me to
say.)

'Ah! Miss Walker, do come in, Nicholas is
just here waiting for you. I'm Miss Holsten,
Nicholas's Arithmetic teacher.' That was it!
She was one of the teachers who had come
looking for Nicholas on the night of the
Allentide party! I went a bit red, but then
I remembered that although I'd seen her, she
hadn't seen me.

I spotted Nicholas sitting in the hall. He
was dressed in his school uniform as usual,
but he looked cleaner and his hair was
smoothed down. He still looked a bit pale,
but a lot better than last time I saw him. He
jumped up when he saw me and walked towards
me. A pretty lady with soft brown hair, who
had been sitting next to him, also walked
towards me and held out her hand for me to
shake. I'd been practising with Uncle Ray so
I knew what to do. I gripped her hand firmly
but not too hard, and moved it up and down
three times. Uncle Ray says a firm handshake
gives a good impression.

'Hello Eleanor, I'm Mrs Worthington,
Nicholas's mother,' she said, smiling. 'I'm
very pleased to meet you. Nicholas has told

me a lot about you. I'm so pleased he has
made such a good friend.' Which was really
nice considering that I had dragged Nicholas
half-way round Cornwall and almost caused him
to freeze to death.

'Good afternoon Mrs Worthington,' I said
politely in my poshest voice. (Uncle Ray's
advice.)

'Nicholas, why don't you take Eleanor into
the dining hall now? I hope you both have a
lovely afternoon.'

'Why did you speak in that silly voice?'
Nicholas said crossly to me, dragging me
along the corridor.

'I'm trying to speak nicely, like you,' I
said.

'Well don't,' he said. 'I like the way you
speak.'

The dining hall was incredible. The ceiling
was almost as high as the sky and the walls
were covered in wooden carvings. It had been
decorated with holly and there were lit
candles everywhere. It looked really
magical! There were lots of boys dressed in
uniform like Nicholas sitting at tables,
chattering and laughing with their families.

We sat down at a little table covered with
a red and green tartan tablecloth. Then a
lady came with some tea in a silver teapot,
and another lady came with sandwiches and

236

cakes on a tall cake stand. My eyes nearly burst from their sockets!

'Are they all for us?' I asked.
Nicholas grinned. 'It looks like it. We don't usually eat as well as this. It must be in your honour!'

Once we were stuffed, Nicholas showed me around the school. We went upstairs to where the classrooms were, and then outside to the field where they played football.

'You're really lucky to have all this space,' I said.

'Yes,' Nicholas agreed. 'I didn't think so before, but now Mother is here with me, everything's going to be so much better. I don't have to try and get expelled anymore, so I won't be getting into any more trouble!' My heart sank a bit when he said that. I quite liked Nicholas when he was getting into trouble. I was pleased that things had worked out so well for him, but he wouldn't need me now. I felt a bit left out.

'Will you be allowed to see me again? I expect your mum will think I'm a bad influence and I might get you into more trouble.'

'Don't worry Eleanor,' he said. 'Mother has every other Sunday afternoon off and she says she'll bring me to see you. You can't get rid of me that easily.'

I laughed and gave him a little punch on the arm. 'Good, I'm glad.' Although it wouldn't be as much fun as leaving secret messages at the gap in the fence. I felt a bit sad, but I was happy for Nicholas now that he had his mum with him all the time.

Frank and I still hadn't heard from *our* mum. There was no time now as the postman had been that morning and wouldn't come again until after Christmas. I wasn't bothered about a present, but it would have been nice to have received a card to show that she'd been thinking about us. Perhaps it had been lost in the post.

Uncle Ray was waiting at the bottom of the steps for me. I turned to Nicholas. 'Happy Christmas Nicholas. Oh, I nearly forgot. I made you a card.' I took it out of my shoulder bag.

'Gosh, thanks Eleanor,' he said. 'And I've got a present for you.' He put a small envelope in my hand. 'You can open it now if you like.' I didn't need to be told twice.

It was two Ovaltiney discs with the names and addresses filled in. One of the names was Nicholas Worthington, and the other one was Charles Richardson.

'Charles is the boy I sit next to in class,' Nicholas said. 'He wants to be an Ovaltiney too. Now you can become an

238

Ovaltiney senior member and get a Silver Star. And there's even a stamp in there for you to send the discs off.'
I gasped in amazement. 'How did you manage it? You don't have Ovaltine at school!
Nicholas laughed. 'Mother arranged it for me. I made her buy lots of Ovaltine and she saved the paper discs in the lids. Apparently she's grown quite fond of drinking it now.'
It was the best Christmas present ever.

This is what I will ACTUALLY be getting

Evening:
'Did you have a good time at the ball, Cinderella?' Uncle Ray asked as I sat next to him on the cart, clutching my present.
'Yes, thank you, coachman,' I replied in my grand voice.
He seemed to find that really funny. 'You've changed a lot since you first came to us, Nellie,' he said. 'Your people back home would find it hard to recognise you.'
I know I've changed a lot. I'm much taller and my knee isn't swollen any more. I don't get styes in my eye now and my cheeks are always rosy. Aunty Mabel said it's because

I'm outside so much. I'm not so skinny
either. Aunty Mabel's wonderful food has
seen to that.

'Are you happy staying with us, Nellie?'
Uncle Ray asked. I looked at him. He was in
a funny mood tonight.

'Of course I am,' I said. 'I love staying
with you, Uncle Ray.' And it was true.
Living in the country was a million times
different to being in London. I love the
green fields and the wild flowers, and being
able to walk with just the sounds of the
birds to listen to. If it wasn't for Mum I
wouldn't ever want to go back to London.

My eyes filled with tears again when I
thought of Mum. Why had she forgotten about
us? Perhaps she was ill and couldn't write?
Or even worse, what if they'd been bombed
again, and this time she hadn't escaped? I
began to feel sick with fear. And what about
our Maureen? I hadn't thought about her for
ages, nor the twins and the baby. What if
they were all hurt in a hospital somewhere?

'Uncle Ray, do you think my mum's all
right?' I whispered. 'I haven't heard from
her for a while.'
Uncle Ray didn't look worried at all. 'I'll
bet my big toe that she's all right, Nellie,'
he said grinning a silly grin. He really was
being odd.

Sunnyvale Farm was in complete darkness
when we got back. The blackout curtains had
been drawn. The light of the full moon lit up
the snow around the farmhouse. It looked
really pretty.

Flossie came out to greet us, barking and
going beserk, as usual, followed by Aunty
Mabel, who was looking extremely smart in her
best dress, which was not usual. She was
looking very pleased about something. Then
Frank came out, also looking smart and
grinning all over his face. What was
happening? Was there some sort of party
going on?

'Off you go, Cinderella,' Uncle Ray was
saying. 'Your fairy godmother has granted
your wish.'

I got down from the cart and walked slowly
towards the farmhouse. I heard a baby crying
from inside. Then suddenly two little boys
came charging out towards me.

'Our Nellie, our Nellie!' they shrieked
excitedly. 'It's us, we're here! We've come
to see you!' And they threw themselves at
me, nearly knocking me to the ground.

'Peter, Paul! What are you …?' I was
flabbergasted. They flung their arms around
my neck as if they would never let me go.

'We're your Christmas present!' they
laughed.

'They wanted to wrap themselves up,' said
our Maureen as she came out of the door. But

she didn't look quite like our Maureen. She
had grown up. Still quite thin, but as
beautiful as ever, and much taller. She
pulled the twins off me and hugged me,
smiling. 'Mum said they're not to make idiots
of themselves in front of strangers.'
My stomach gave a lurch.
  'MUM?'
 Maureen nodded towards the house.   'She's
inside, waiting for you. She said she wanted
you to herself. Go on in, our Nellie, she's
dying to see you.'

It's hard to describe how I felt when I saw
my lovely mum after such a long time. In
fact, I'm not even going to try. It's so
very, very marvellous and private.
What we said to each other and what we did
doesn't belong in this journal, but it will
stay in my heart and my memory for as long as
I live.

  Thank you for reading my journal. I hope
you enjoyed it.

with love
from Nellie
xxx

DESERT HERO cont...

"What are your plans now, Tex?" Bella asked.
Tex frowned. "Although Mad Man is locked up
in the town jail, nothing's changed," he said
gloomily. "I still don't have any money to buy
my ranch."

Suddenly the saloon door burst open and the
sheriff ran in. "I just heard from the judge.
There's a reward of $1000 for the capture of
Mad Man McBlaine, and you deserve that reward,
Tex!"

"You're a rich man, Tex!" Bella shrieked.
"You've got enough for ten cattle ranches
now!"

Tex smiled. His dream had finally come
true, and it couldn't have happened without
his new friends.

"We're a team," he said to Bella. "The ranch
is yours as well. Dave, there's enough money
for you to build a big, posh hotel. And you,
Sheriff, you can have free beef for the rest of
your days. I might be rich but friendship is
worth more than money can buy!"

THE END

I've put this in so that you don't need to keep flicking through the pages to find it again, but don't tell anyone because it's supposed to be very hush hush.

A=2, B=4, C=6, D=8, E=10, F=12, G=14, H=16,
I=18, J=20, K=22, L=24, M=26, N=28, O=30,
P=32, Q=34, R=36, S=38, T=40, U=42, V=44,
W=46, X=48, Y=50, Z=52

You might like to try some of the recipes mentioned in my journal.

BREAD PUDDING

Approximately 1½ loaves white bread, soaked in water in a large bowl until soft and squidgy (around 1 hour). Mum used a clean washing up bowl.
1 oz plain flour
3 oz shredded suet (beef or vegetable)
1 pot mixed spice
4 oz sugar

8 oz   dried fruit. (I prefer sultanas)
1.   Pick up large pieces of the soaked bread and squeeze all of the water out into the sink. Put the squeezed bread on a dry chopping board.
2.   Tip out the remaining water into the sink and put the squeezed bread back into the bowl.

3.   Add all the rest of the ingredients and mix in with your hands until everything is mixed together.
4.   Add the mixture into a large, greased pie dish or roasting dish.
5.   Bake for 1-2 hours at 180 degrees C. until slightly crispy on top.
6.   Sprinkle some more sugar on top while still warm.
7.   Cut into squares while still warm and eat. It's also delicious cold.

ALLANTIDE APPLE CAKE

Try and peel the apple in one go, throw the peel over your shoulder and it will form the initial of the person you will marry.

220 g plain flour
120g butter
220g currants
1 tsp ground ginger
60g mixed peel

1 tsp cinnamon

1 tsp bicarbonate of soda

5 tbsp full fat milk

2 beaten eggs

2 dessert apples, peeled and very thinly sliced (you can keep in them water to stop them from going brown, but make sure you drain them thoroughly when you want to use them.)

20g dark brown sugar to decorate

20 cm cake tin

1. Preheat the oven to 150 deg C.
2. Thoroughly grease cake tin.
3. Rub flour and butter together.
4. Put into a mixing bowl and add the rest of the dry ingredients.
5. Add beaten eggs.
6. Mix milk and bicarbonate of soda together, and add to the dry mixture, adding a little more milk if necessary – the mixture should drop softly off the spoon.
7. Put half the mixture into the tin, and then lay on the sliced apple on the mixture. Then add the rest of the mixture.
8. Sprinkle the sugar on top.
9. Bake in the oven for about an hour, until golden brown on top, and cooked through.

Lovely served with Cornish clotted cream!

CORNISH PASTIES

Shortcrust Pastry (or you could buy ready-made pastry)

- 500 g strong bread flour (it is important to use a stronger flour than normal as you need the extra strength in the gluten to produce strong pliable pastry)
- 120 g lard or white shortening
- 125 g Cornish butter
- 1 tsp salt
- 175 ml cold water

FOR THE FILLING

- 400 g good quality beef skirt, cut into cubes
- 300 g potato, peeled and diced
- 150 g swede, peeled and diced
- 150 g onion, peeled and sliced
- Salt & pepper to taste
- Beaten egg or milk to glaze

METHOD

1. Add the salt to the flour in a large mixing bowl.
2. Rub the two types of fat lightly into flour until it resembles breadcrumbs.

3. Add water, bring the mixture together and knead until the pastry becomes elastic. This will take longer than normal pastry but it gives the pastry the strength that is needed to hold the filling and retain a good shape. This can also be done in a food mixer.

4. Cover with cling film and leave to rest for 3 hours in the fridge. This is a very important stage as it is almost impossible to roll and shape the pastry when fresh.

5. Roll out the pastry and cut into circles approx. 20cm diameter. A side plate is an ideal size to use as a guide.

6. Layer the vegetables and meat on top of the pastry, adding plenty of seasoning.

7. Bring the pastry around and crimp the edges together. Glaze with beaten egg or an egg and milk mixture.

8. Bake at 165 degrees C (fan oven) for about 50 – 55 minutes until golden.

Here are the messages Nicholas and I wrote just in case you don't want to work them out.

<u>Message No. 1</u>
Hello everyone

<u>Message No. 2</u>
Apple pie in your eye
Flick it out and watch it fly

<u>Message No. 3</u>
Meet me here Tuesday after school. It is a matter of life and death.

<u>Message No. 4</u>
I am still here

<u>Message No. 5</u>
Meet me in our camp next Saturday after breakfast.

ACKNOWLEDGEMENTS

Researching and writing this book has been a four year obsession and a complete joy, so I would like to thank some marvellous people who helped make it happen.

My wonderful husband, Brian Morris, for his love and encouragement.

My proof readers and critics, Debbie Holland and Jean Holland. (Jeannie can spot a misplaced apostrophe a mile away.)

My young critics, who were armed with the early manuscript, highlight markers and smiley face stickers, Daisy and Esther. Thank you for your input and enthusiasm.

To Nikko, a fellow stallholder at Chartham Farmers' Market who told me many stories of his childhood and was the inspiration behind Nellie's friend, Nicholas. His mother actually did become the house mother at the boarding school Nikko was evacuated to.

To my sorely missed Popsy, Dave Holland, who was an avid WW2 historian, and dragged his children around castles and museums at every opportunity.

But most of all, an enormous thank you to my amazing mum, Anne Holland, nee Willsher whose stories and memories have made up the bulk of this book.   She is of course, Nellie, and is still as full of fun and energy as she ever was.

Some of the sources of my research:

<u>Places I visited</u>
The Imperial War Museum, London
The Old Forge, Sittingbourne

<u>Books I read</u>
No Time to Say Goodbye by Ben Wicks
A Point of Arrival by Chaim Bermant

I also dipped in and out of many other books and TV programmes that sparked off ideas in my head.

<u>Websites I explored</u>
Cornishculture.co.uk
Cornwallinformation.co.uk
bbc.co.uk WW2 People's War
iwm.org

More recently I discovered a brilliant Facebook page, The British Evacuees Association, and Doreen Simson has been a great help confirming details and sharing her story with me.

Printed in Great Britain
by Amazon